DAEDALUS
AND
THE MINOTAUR

DAEDALUS AND THE MINOTAUR

TALES OF ANCIENT LANDS SERIES

5/00 J292

Written by Priscilla Galloway
Illustrated by Normand Cousineau

Annick Press Ltd.
Toronto • New York

Annick Press Ltd.

Annick Press gratefully acknowledges the support of the Canada Council
and the Ontario Arts Council.

Cataloguing in Publication Data
Galloway, Priscilla, 1930-
Daedalus and the minotaur

(Tales of ancient lands)
ISBN 1-55037-459-1 (bound)   ISBN 1-55037-458-3 (pbk.)

1. Daedalus (Greek mythology) - Juvenile fiction.
2. Icarus (Greek mythology) - Juvenile fiction.
I. Cousineau, Normand. II. Title. III. Series: Galloway, Priscilla, 1930- . Tales of ancient lands.

PS8563.A45D33 1997   jC813'.54   C97-930796-1   PZ8.1.G34Da 1997

The art in this book was rendered in ink and gouache.
The text was typeset in Perpetua and Lithos.

Distributed in Canada by: Firefly Books Ltd.
3680 Victoria Park Avenue, Willowdale, ON M2H 3K1

Published in the U.S.A. by Annick Press (U.S.) Ltd.
Distributed in the U.S.A. by: Firefly Books (U.S.) Inc.
P.O. Box 1338, Ellicott Station, Buffalo, NY 14205

Printed and bound in Canada by Metropole Litho, Montréal

"*I do not think there is any thrill that
can go through the human heart like
that felt by the inventor as he sees some
creation of the brain unfolding to success…
Such emotions make a man forget food,
sleep, friends, love, everything.*"

Nikola Tesla, 1896.

To my son Walt,
and to the memory of Nikola Tesla.

P.G.

À Sylvie pour Thomas, lui qui m'a donné des ailes.
Merci à Rita et Gisèle.

N.C.

CONTENTS

MT. OLYMPUS

TROY

AEGEAN SEA

GREECE

CALYDON

DELPHI

ITHACA

ATHENS

MYCENAE

ASIA MINOR

LACONIA

SPARTA

MEDITERRANEAN SEA

TO CYCLOPS

CRETE

CHARACTERS
IN THIS STORY

DAEDALUS (Ded' uh lus), the great inventor, architect and builder

ICARUS (Ik' uh rus), his son

MENA (Mee' nuh), servant of Daedalus

STEPHANOS (Steff ah' nus), servant of Daedalus

PASSIFAY (Pass' if ay), the queen at Knossos (Noss' us) on the island of Crete

MINOS (My' nus), the king at Knossos

MINOTAUR (Min' uh tor), a royal child who is hidden away

ARIADNE (A ree ad' nee), daughter of the king and queen

HEPHAESTUS (Hee fest' us), the lame god, god of artisans and builders, remote ancestor of Daedalus

APOLLON (A' poll un), brother of Daedalus

AMASIA (A may' see uh), wife of Apollon

HEBE (Hee' bee), artisan, inventor, friend of Daedalus

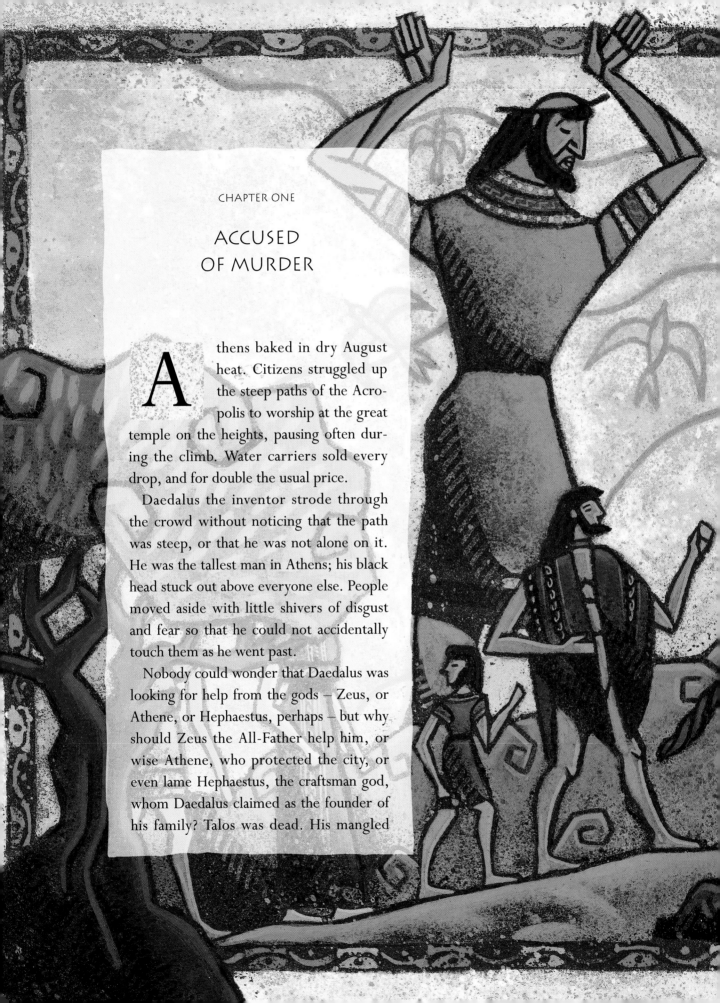

CHAPTER ONE

ACCUSED
OF MURDER

Athens baked in dry August heat. Citizens struggled up the steep paths of the Acropolis to worship at the great temple on the heights, pausing often during the climb. Water carriers sold every drop, and for double the usual price.

Daedalus the inventor strode through the crowd without noticing that the path was steep, or that he was not alone on it. He was the tallest man in Athens; his black head stuck out above everyone else. People moved aside with little shivers of disgust and fear so that he could not accidentally touch them as he went past.

Nobody could wonder that Daedalus was looking for help from the gods – Zeus, or Athene, or Hephaestus, perhaps – but why should Zeus the All-Father help him, or wise Athene, who protected the city, or even lame Hephaestus, the craftsman god, whom Daedalus claimed as the founder of his family? Talos was dead. His mangled

body had been found at the foot of the cliff, obviously thrown down there from the top, and Daedalus was suspected of murdering him, out of jealousy. His own nephew, his own apprentice!

Even before Talos had died so horribly, the citizens of Athens had been afraid of Daedalus. Everybody knew he had superhuman powers. You only had to look at him, taller and skinnier than anybody else, with black hair that sprang out around his head like a halo, and those piercing bright blue eyes! Rumours flew in the wake of Talos's death, and the stories grew with every telling.

"They went up the hill together, didn't they."

"Two men went up, but only one came back."

"Arrest Daedalus, then. What are they waiting for? He's a clever man, but this is Athens: he can't get away with murder!"

The morning air was still, gathering ever more heat. Daedalus strode onward, lost in painful thought. Suddenly a stone hit his back, then several small pebbles pelted against his shoulders. His head jerked up, and he turned angrily around. He saw only black looks and heard only curses. Daedalus turned again, his actions as quick as his thoughts. A narrow path branched off from the main way, and he swung into it. This was no day for the great temple. He would seek a small, secluded shrine.

Nobody followed him, and he was soon once more focused inwards. Tears wet his cheeks, and he wiped them away with slim, strong, square-tipped fingers, remembering Talos's hands, so much like his own. When he reached the shrine, he sat down on the brown summer grass, head on his knees.

People cannot be trusted, he told himself. They leave you. They betray you. They die. I can't depend on anybody. What can I trust?

I can trust my work. When I boil water, it always turns to steam. When I sharpen my bronze blade, it takes an edge. If I cut a piece of wood, it stays cut. When I create something new, it exists. If I do not change it, it does not change.

The air shimmered with heat. An hour went by, but Daedalus did not move. He thought about Talos, but soon his thoughts moved to Dania, his young wife who had died. Like most Athenians, Daedalus had waited until he was almost thirty before taking a wife, and had married, according to custom, a girl just turned fifteen. Dania was eager to obey and ready to be taught. Alas, Daedalus found her slow, clumsy, stupid, in every way the opposite of Talos. Dania bored him to death. When she became pregnant, Daedalus thankfully sacrificed a bullock on the altar of Hera. He had done his duty by Dania; now let her care for her child. He prayed she would bear a son.

The son was born, a healthy, beautiful child. Daedalus had been surprised and amused to find himself like other fathers: his heart swelled with joy and pride. He put the baby's cradle in his workshop, but he would not allow Dania to come there to rock it. Talos had devised a system of cogs and gears. One push every now and again would set the cradle swinging for hours. Dania saw the contraption once. "Hera save me," she'd cried, "he'll fall out and be killed." The cradle did not tip over, however, and baby Icarus spent most  of each day in the busy room. When he cried, their servant Mena took him to his mother to be nursed, then brought him back again.

Daedalus had had no previous experience of babies, and he marvelled at the physical properties of this one. He could spend hours examining the tiny fingers, the intricate whorls of the minuscule ears, and the dark blue eyes, mirrors of his own. Then Daedalus laughed in delight, and Icarus gurgled happily in response.

Daedalus had spent less time with the little fellow as he grew. Placed on the floor, Icarus began to roll, then to creep. He was seven months old when he fell out of the cradle the first time, but the second fall came less

than a week later. Within a few days, the baby had learned to climb out, setting the cradle rocking wildly. He had crept about the cluttered workshop and begun to pull himself up, using anything he could reach. Talos jumped to stop the cradle gears one day just before the tiny hand was caught. He shuddered. "Daedalus, that was too close. What if he'd got his hand crushed? Next time I might not see him soon enough."

"You're right." Daedalus looked down at the boy, his fingers drumming on the table. He remembered clearly that he had been painting a dragonfly, trying to catch with his brush and colours every detail of its shimmering wings. A vision of Icarus, his hand crushed and bleeding, superimposed itself on his vision of the fragile dragonfly.

Daedalus had shaken his head in frustration. Icarus was growing, changing right under his eyes. Daedalus had noticed, of course, but without paying attention. Clearly, Icarus had become a danger, not only to himself but also to the delicate models, the fragile pots and beakers, and the clay tablets where Daedalus scratched his notes. For Daedalus, to see a problem was to act on it. But what should be done?

"Icarus, you're interrupting my work," he had announced solemnly. Icarus laughed and held out his arms to be picked up. Daedalus swung him up in the air. The problem had an easy solution after all. He handed the child to Talos. "Take him to his mother," Daedalus said. "Yes, it's time he spent more time with her."

Had he missed the boy? Not really. Once more, he was able to focus completely on his work, without a tiny hand tugging at his tunic, or a little babbling voice whose syllables he could not quite understand. It had been a relief.

Dania had laughed for joy. Daedalus never guessed her terror lest Icarus, having been given to her, might be as quickly snatched away again. As the months passed, Dania gained confidence. From feeding and bathing her son and hiding with him in corners of the house, she slowly came into the

open. She and Icarus taught each other to play.

Then one day Mena fainted in the kitchen. Daedalus remembered how Dania stayed up with her, putting cool cloths on her forehead. Three days later, Dania too became flushed and dizzy. Daedalus felt his wife's rosy cheek. "You're burning up, Dania," he'd said. "Go to bed. Where's Stephanos?" He looked around for their other servant. "Talos, get him to move the boy's bed into our workroom. Icarus can sleep there until his mother is healthy again."

Mena was well enough to care for her mistress, bathing Dania in cool water, then covering the fevered body with wet linen. Stephanos was sent to fetch the doctor, who opened a vein in Dania's arm and drew off a quantity of blood. It was no use. Within a day, Dania was delirious. Within a week, she was dead. Mena took charge of Icarus.

"I miss Dania," Talos said abruptly, a month or so after her death. "When she was playing with Icarus, she had such a happy laugh."

ᐁᐁᐁᐁ

Talos is dead, Daedalus told himself. So is Dania. He shook his head angrily, as if he could shake away these memories. He wiped his sweaty face. He missed Talos dreadfully – Dania too, although he had not missed her when Talos was alive. Now, he too missed her laughter.

Suddenly, a voice broke in on his reverie. "Daedalus, here you are. The gods be thanked!" The speaker puffed and panted, then went on. "They told me at your house where to search, but it's taken hours. I was afraid I'd missed you."

Slowly Daedalus looked up. He knew from the first word that the speaker was his brother, father of the young man who had died. Apollon's face was puffy with weeping. Daedalus scrambled to his feet. He and Apollon clung to each other.

"You were looking for me?" Daedalus asked grimly. "Good news, I wonder, or is it bad?"

Big tears brimmed at once in Apollon's eyes. He looked wearily at the ground. "It's all bad news, these days," he sighed.

"Tell me."

"Amasia wants me to arrest you and take you before the archon to be tried for murder. Zeus defend me, Daedalus, my own wife! My own brother!" He lifted despairing eyes.

"She believed me earlier. You both did."

"She doesn't believe you now. She wouldn't listen to the gossip at first. You must know how it goes: 'The pupil has surpassed his master, and Daedalus is eaten up with jealousy.' 'That's crazy talk,' Amasia used to say. But then a friend brought her another tale. 'I know a man who saw the push,' says her friend. 'Daedalus did it.'" Apollon felt his lips quivering.

"Zeus protect me from liars!" Daedalus shook with rage and frustration. "And you, brother, what do you believe?"

Apollon looked up at his tall brother, blinking away his tears. His voice was low, but steady. "I know you, Daedalus. You don't have a jealous bone in your body. You wouldn't kill anyone for jealousy, especially a boy you loved like Talos."

As he spoke, however, a horrid thought rose in his mind. Yes, Daedalus, I know you. It's your work that matters, nothing else. If Talos was a threat to your work, what would you do? ... No, you wouldn't kill him, how can I think something so dreadful? Apollon shook his head.

"What was I saying?" he went on. "I believe you, Daedalus, of course I do. But Amasia doesn't know you the way I do. You're not her brother. Our son has been killed, her only child. 'Let Atropos come for Daedalus with her shears,' she screams. 'Let the old witch cut off his life thread. I'll dance in his blood.'"

Daedalus shuddered. "I hope Atropos is not listening," he said.

"I hope not as well, for Amasia's sake as much as yours. She's tempting the fates." Apollon shivered.

"A murder suit from my own brother! If you arrest me, everybody will be sure the stories are true. Talos's death is a tragedy, for you and for me as well as Amasia. Do you want to make it worse than it is already? Who rules your household, Apollon? You must tell your wife you won't do it."

"I could tell her that. Certainly." Apollon's square face was grey with wretchedness. "And then she'd hate me. Probably for ever. Daedalus, I love my wife."

"Arrest me then, and be done with it." Daedalus was shaking with horror and rage. He held out his hands, as if waiting for his brother to tie them up.

"No," said Apollon. He tried to say more, but choked on the words. He turned away.

Daedalus put out a hand and drew it back again. He sat down on a rock with his back to the little shrine. My son Icarus is alive, he thought dully.

The thought brought him no joy.

At last Apollon looked at him. His voice was bleak. "You must leave Athens, Daedalus. It's the only way."

"Leave Athens!" The thought had been weighing on Daedalus for days, ever since the whispering began, but it was dreadful to hear it spoken aloud. To a citizen of Athens, there was little to choose between banishment and death.

"Go to Crete," Apollon continued. "King Minos has invited you, more than once. You will be honoured in the great palace."

"And I, an Athenian citizen, must work for a tyrant?" Daedalus stiffened. A pulse throbbed at his temple. Rage darkened his deep blue eyes.

Apollon looked at his brother's scarlet face, at the tense body and clenched fists. He forced himself to reply calmly. "Yes," he returned, "unless you can think of some other way. I can't. Don't put us through a trial here, Daedalus. I do not think I could bear it." He paused, gathering strength. "The gods have brought a Cretan ship to our harbour, even though it's late in the season. She anchored yesterday. I've sent a messenger to book your passage. I beg you, brother, give thanks, as I do, and sail with her."

Apollon's entreaty sucked the rage out of Daedalus as quickly as it had risen. In the past, King Minos had offered wealth, power, protection, men and materials without limit, but Daedalus had never been tempted. In Crete, he would be the king's servant, building, inventing, creating what his master desired. If he opposed the royal will in Crete, there would be no trial.

"You had no business booking passage without talking to me," Daedalus said petulantly, and at once felt ashamed of himself. "Besides, the captain won't want to linger while I make ready."

Apollon's voice was stronger. "If 'making ready' means packing everything in the house, you have no time for it. In your name, I sent Icarus and

Mena off to the harbour this morning. They will be on board the Cretan ship in an hour or two. Stephanos is only waiting to see what you want him to carry. You're a father, Daedalus. If you won't think of yourself, or Amasia, or me, if I may say so, think of your boy. Get up, the tide won't wait."

Daedalus rose wearily to his feet. Now Icarus would never be a citizen of Athens – because Talos had been killed.

How could anyone say Daedalus had caused that death? How dare they say it? And for jealousy! Daedalus had been thrilled over Talos's brilliant idea for the saw. He had helped cut the metal teeth for the very first saw Talos made, and had rejoiced that the invention would make his nephew famous.

He and Talos had never been rivals; rather, they had inspired each other. Talos had shared his uncle's dream of flying, and Daedalus had kindled the spark of Talos's obsession to build a mechanical man. Daedalus constantly watched flying creatures of every kind, from the tiny dragonflies to the great eagles that soared above him, floating high and higher, though scarcely moving their wings. He devised kites and flew them on the hilltops, trying to get them to glide and soar like birds. He dissected the bodies of dead birds, bees and butterflies, with particular attention to the structure of their wings. He pulled out birds' feathers and examined the silken down. With a small version of Talos's invention, he sawed off cross-sections of bird bones.

Talos was equally devoted to his own major project. The gears and cogs that rocked baby Icarus's cradle had been designed to move the legs of the mechanical man.

"Surely a mechanical man could do a servant's work," Daedalus had said. "Such a creature would never need to rest. We'd have to find something different for Stephanos to do."

Talos had let out his breath in a long sigh. "The old stories say Hephaestus

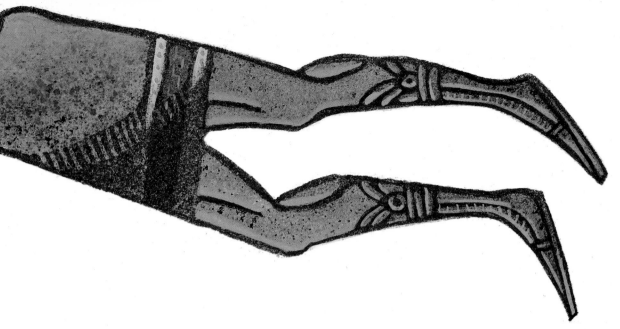

made a mechanical man to stoke his furnaces, and golden handmaids to serve at his table. Some men would accuse me of deadly pride, trying to imitate the gods."

Daedalus shivered now, remembering what Talos had said next. Could the lame god Hephaestus himself have hurled Talos to his death? Talos had boasted, "Uncle, we'll go our godly ancestor Hephaestus one better: our mechanical man will perform many tasks, not just one. I have a name for this creature: android."

"Android. Like a man, but not a living being."

"Not a thinking being," Talos had added. "Uncle," he'd continued quietly, "when we have made enough mechanical men, people will be equal to the gods!"

A cold wind from the little shrine behind him seemed to blow on Daedalus. Where he stood, looking at his brother without really seeing him, the heat was sucked out of the sun. Daedalus had a vision of Hephaestus at his forge, hammering out armour of bronze inlaid with silver. As Daedalus watched, the lame god put down his hammer. Talos's words echoed: People will be equal to the gods. The god's face seemed to be carved from stone, yet Daedalus felt in his inmost being Hephaestus's mounting rage.

Time bounced back and forward like a ball, and Daedalus listened again to every boast Talos had made, overlaid with the red-hot anger of the god. He watched while Talos carved wood and snipped metal, while each succes-

sive version of the android moved less stiffly. At last Talos had completed a creature of wood and metal that moved on two legs and could hold a wine cup steady in its silver hands. "Uncle," he'd called, ready to show his newest work.

Daedalus had never seen the android that now appeared in his vision. Why not? Whenever Talos finished something new, he had always rushed to show it to Daedalus. Again, his vision showed the answer. Hephaestus had taken his place, and Talos was fooled. The disguise was perfect: Daedalus could see his own face as if it were a mask, and through his face the impassive face of the god.

Talos had never doubted he was talking to Daedalus, so when his uncle had suggested they walk together up the Acropolis hill, the young man had stood up at once. He was not nervous, even when they stood together at the top of the steepest cliff. There, however, Hephaestus had taken his own terrible form.

"Come, Boreas," he had called, in a voice of thunder, and the north wind had come. Talos had trembled then, as the wind roared about him.

Daedalus watched in horror. He stared helplessly as the god pointed, and the wind picked up Talos, sucked him out into the void, and let him go. Daedalus's legs buckled. He sank down with bowed head and slumped shoulders on the rock in front of his brother. Sweat gathered in his armpits. His head throbbed. With this vision Hephaestus sent him a clear message: men are not gods, no matter what they may create.

∾∾∾

"What's the matter with you?" Daedalus heard Apollon's anxious voice as if from a great distance. "Say something, can't you?" his brother asked. "You haven't heard a thing I've said for the last ten minutes. What's wrong? You look like death."

Daedalus stared up at his brother. If the vision he had seen was true, then he was partly guilty of Talos's death. He had never tried to curb his nephew's pride. He had never reproached him for saying that humans would in time be equal to the gods. Leaving Athens was no less a wrench, but staying was impossible.

Daedalus struggled with the new information. I was not there when Talos died, he reminded himself, but it makes no difference. Hephaestus looked exactly like me. Who knows how many people saw him? Many witnesses may come forward to say so. They will be convincing; they know what they saw. In the end, even Apollon will not be able to believe that all of them are liars.

He stared up at his brother. Their features were very different, but they had the same stubborn chin. Daedalus was first to drop his eyes. "We'll go down the mountain," he mumbled. "I'll decide everything at the bottom."

"Don't you understand me yet?" Apollon was exasperated. "If you do not leave, I will take you to court for murder. It would be the hardest thing I've ever done. But if you force me to choose between my wife and my brother, I warn you one more time, I will choose my wife. What are you going to do?"

Daedalus leaped to his feet. "You choose your wife, Apollon," he snapped. "Now get out of my way. You're no brother of mine." His long legs took him down the steep path at a furious pace. The sun burned, hot enough to drive a man out of his senses. At his hairline, and under his short tunic, Daedalus dripped with sweat.

About halfway down the Acropolis, the little path merged back into the main thoroughfare. Once again people drew aside as the tall figure strode along like a ship cutting through waves. Here and there a man or woman shook a clenched fist. The muttering grew louder as Daedalus plunged forward, and the people drew closer together. At length Daedalus found himself facing a solid wall of screaming, jeering men and women. His eyes

darted about, looking nervously for the first arm raised to throw a stone. He turned. Perhaps behind him the mass of humanity would be thinner. At once he saw Apollon pushing his way through the mob.

"Apollon, Apollon," came the cries. "Kill the murderer," yelled a man, "kill Daedalus." Other voices took up the cry. People bent to pick up stones.

Daedalus braced himself. What would his brother do?

"That's enough," Apollon shouted, swaying a little as if he had spent the day swilling wine at the taverna. "You want a fight – no, no, I don't fight with my brother. Go home, everybody. It's dinner time, and the children are hungry. Go home."

One man threw a rock. His aim was good. The missile hit Daedalus on the shoulder. Daedalus stooped, looking for his own ammunition. Apollon pushed forward. The second rock caught Apollon on the forehead. He staggered, although he did not yet feel any pain. His raised hand came away warm with blood. The shouting died.

"Go home," repeated Apollon quietly. "Daedalus, follow me." He turned, staggering a little. Daedalus offered an arm, but Apollon shook it off and started to walk back the way he had come. Men and women moved out of his way. The hot sun beat down on their heads. Even the wind was quiet.

Like a tall ship behind a squat tug, Daedalus followed his brother. What could he say? Nothing, except to thank him and accept his help.

"That's all right, then," said Apollon gruffly. "The way that crowd behaved, it's obvious you can't go home to pack. You get on to the harbour. I'll go to your house. Tell me what you want the most – drawings, models. Stephanos and I will bring what we can."

"Will you be all right? I'm not so angry any more."

"I'm glad of that," said Apollon. "Thanks to you, Amasia and I will be able to grieve for our son together. Time heals, they say, though right now I don't believe it." He shrugged. "The gods know the future, but we mor-

tals do not." He and Daedalus held each other in a long embrace, then Apollon turned aside.

Daedalus strode on. He did not look back. He walked through the long dusk into the night. The moon was almost full. When he reached Piraeus Harbour at last, the tide was coming in. Much of the sandy beach was covered. Many small boats were drawn up on the shore. One, however, was half in and half out of the water. Daedalus's sandals crunched in the sand as he approached it. Suddenly, a man sat up. "Bound for Crete?" he asked.

"Yes," replied Daedalus.

"You're the father?" asked the man, rubbing his eyes. Daedalus nodded. "Help me shove off, then. Your boy and the woman are already on board." He pointed, and Daedalus looked. The setting moon threw a long silver-golden path across the quiet water toward the Cretan ship where she rode at anchor, a black shape against the sky.

CHAPTER TWO

A DANGEROUS REFUGE

Daedalus was devoutly thankful when the Cretan harbour at Nirou Chani came in sight. This was his first voyage, but he had seen at once that the ship's sail did a poor job when the wind changed, and he was appalled by the clumsy steering oar. If he could give his attention to these problems, he could surely design something better. Unfortunately, Stephanos had been seasick the whole time, and Daedalus and Mena had spent almost all their waking hours keeping track of Icarus. "How can one three-year-old be a full-time job for both of us?" he grumbled.

The ship from Athens dropped anchor amid dozens of other vessels, sailors shouted greetings back and forth, and a little boat ferried the passengers and their belongings ashore. Stephanos began to revive as soon as his feet touched the ground, though all the party went lurching about, feeling the land move under them as if they were still riding the waves.

Daedalus, whose legs were steadiest, found an ox-cart big enough for four people and the mountain of possessions that Apollon had managed to put aboard in Athens. They were bound for the great city of Knossos, where King Minos ruled.

"Send a runner ahead to announce my arrival," Daedalus commanded. He looked about him, excited but uneasy. His stomach had formed itself into a tight ball of tension. Would he and his son be welcome here? Automatically, he looked for the child.

Icarus was struggling to get away from Mena. "I'll take him." Daedalus climbed into the cart and held out his arms. Icarus settled against his father's bony frame. Daedalus felt a rush of affection. In one way the sea voyage had been a blessing: he had not spent so much time with Icarus since the child had been a baby.

Icarus pushed against his father's restraining arms. "Stop wriggling, child," commanded Daedalus impatiently. His mind was playing with an adaptation of Talos's android, something along the lines of a mechanical ox. He could almost see it, fast as the wind, clanking along the dusty roads. Daedalus held his child, and let his mind roam free.

The wide road sloped gently upward. The oxen plodded on steadily, drawing the cart and its passengers between airy, prosperous-looking, flat-roofed houses, most of them two stories high. Unlike the houses of Athens, these were set well back from the road and apart from each other. Daedalus could not see any walls, or any evidence of fortifications. Obviously, these people did not live in fear of attack.

Outside the harbour town, the road wound through groves of trees, the afternoon sun glinting on oak leaves beginning to turn yellow, or on the dark olive branches. "Look," screamed Icarus. He pointed, and tried to jump up. Daedalus's arms tightened. On a hill above them, a graceful, horned animal stood for a moment, then turned and bounded away.

"Ibex," grunted the driver. "Not too often you see one around here. A lucky sign, I'd say."

Daedalus would never forget his surprise at the first sight of Knossos. How rich this land must be! How peaceful! How secure! The size of the city awed him. He found out later that it boasted a hundred thousand citizens, ten times more than Athens. The vast city had no walls whatsoever.

Even in Athens, people had heard of King Minos and his magnificent palace. As the ox-cart came nearer, the outline of its walls gradually dominated, then filled, the landscape. The walls were topped by symbolic horns of consecration, and Daedalus at first mistook them for defences. Then he realized he was observing the flat-roofed palace itself. The royal court of Knossos was so powerful that no palisades were needed.

Although no one had had much notice of his arrival, Daedalus was received at the great north gate with honour. Bowing servants escorted him up a wide flight of steps whose central columns tapered toward the bottom. He entered an airy room, bright with frescoes. Daedalus was enchanted. Everything he saw delighted him. An official wearing a huge golden medallion bustled forward, smiling.

"Every true artist is welcome at this court," he said. "You are already famous here, Master Daedalus. I am the royal chamberlain. My secretary Domios will show you to your rooms. Whatever you need for your comfort, you have only to ask."

Daedalus had many questions, starting with: When will I see the king? What will he want of me? Where will I set up my workshop? But this was not the time for questions. He bowed politely, then turned to follow Domios. Tonight, he must settle himself and rest.

The next day, Daedalus fretted but heard nothing. He did not want to leave his rooms in case he was sent for, and he could hardly begin to set up his workroom until he knew what work he was to do. Mena unpacked his wax tablets, and Daedalus sketched birds and kites and mechanical men, each more absurdly fantastic than the one before. Again and again, Mena interrupted her unpacking and sorting to melt the wax so that the tablets could be used again.

Three days went by, with Daedalus becoming angrier every minute. "I have torn my life up to come here," he complained, forgetting that this was not the whole truth, "and this is my reward! The king and queen ignore me!"

Mena was silent, but she was greatly relieved when Domios arrived bearing a loincloth embroidered in silver and the royal invitation to an audience the following day. Daedalus admired the shimmering scrap of fabric but balked at wearing it.

"Will the king be offended if I do not wear his gift?" he asked, staring down from his great height.

"It's not his gift," replied Domios, "but my master's."

"My thanks to your master," Daedalus said firmly. "Please tell him I am Athenian born. I'll keep Athenian dress."

"As you wish, Master Giant," replied Domios, with sparkling eyes. "Most men cling to their own customs, and never more so than in a foreign land. We see all the world's fashions here at court. Wear what pleases you. Nobody will think less of you on that account."

Daedalus was already sweating in his woolen tunic as he followed the chamberlain toward his first royal audience. He entered a large room, crowded with elegant men and women. Two walls were bright with painted scenes; two walls were open, with balconies looking out into the sunlit air.

Daedalus's first major surprise at Knossos had been that city and palace had no walls. His second was that he could not tell who was more important, the king or the queen. In every way that he could see, the queen was equal to the king. They sat side by side. Both were richly dressed. They seemed almost the same age, though Daedalus thought the queen might be slightly older than the king.

Queen Passifay – Daedalus never did manage to pronounce it exactly like a native Cretan – was small and slender, a match for King Minos in physique as well as age. Her laughing face was skilfully painted, her dark eyes blackened with rings of kohl, eyes "as big as a hen's egg," as her admirers liked to say. Even in the short time he had been at court, Daedalus had observed the fashion of high-born women. The queen and all the court ladies flaunted the tight, skimpy bodice and the wide sculptured skirt falling to the ankles. Daedalus hid his disapproval, dismissing sudden memory, sharp as pain, of home. In Athens, a respectable woman wore clothes that covered her body and did not reveal its shape.

The king's dress, and that of the other men, also shocked him. The king wore a golden necklet and a gold-embroidered loincloth, richer than that of the others, but equally lacking in modesty. His head was crowned with plumes.

Daedalus never became comfortable with court fashions. As soon as possible, he changed his woolen tunics for linen, but throughout his years at Knossos he continued to wear Athenian dress.

Stephanos walked behind his master, a wool-wrapped bundle in his arms. The gift was large and heavy, and Daedalus's servant struggled to walk with dignity. He set the mysterious bundle on a table in front of the royal couple. Another servant carried a golden pitcher full of water; a third brought a richly carved silver basin. Proudly, Daedalus unwrapped his gift.

"How pretty," said the queen, bending forward to admire the little birds in their nest, and the mother bird, wings folded, perched above.

Daedalus smiled. The idea for the toy had come to him as he struggled to help Talos with his mechanical man. Daedalus lifted the jug and began to pour water into the sphere below the birds. Suddenly a snake rose from the sphere, threatening the babies in their nest.

The queen was bending over the toy, and the snake almost hit her face. She jumped back, jerking her hands away. Then she tossed her head and stepped forward again.

Daedalus poured more water. At once the mother bird raised her metal wings, ready to attack the snake and protect her babies. The tall man paused dramatically. He checked the position of the silver basin, then opened a plug at the bottom of the sphere. As the water drained, the snake sank back out of sight. With a slight metallic clank, the mother bird folded her wings.

"Ahhhh," sighed the queen.

"Do it again," commanded King Minos. His face was impassive, except for the sparkle in his eyes.

Daedalus did it again. And again. And again. Men and women of the court crowded round. Each time, there was a collective gasp as the snake rose, a chuckle as the mother bird threatened it, and a contented sigh as the water was emptied once more.

Suddenly, a child's voice broke in with, "Mine, mine." Little Icarus banged on the side of the table, trying to reach the toy.

Angrily, Daedalus caught up his son. What was Mena doing, letting him wander?

"Your son?" King Minos already knew the answer.

"Pardon his bad manners," said Daedalus in a low voice.

"Certainly," said the king, but his voice was suddenly frosty. Everyone in the big hall had been laughing. Now all faces were sober. The queen's face had turned dead white. Her nose looked pinched.

"Don't let me see this child again, or it will be the worse for him," she commanded. "Make me something else, Daedalus, something that nobody in the world has seen and touched before."

The court ladies clapped dutifully. The queen gestured, and a dark-haired woman in blue and silver took Icarus by the hand and half-led, half-dragged him toward the door. As she passed Daedalus, she hissed, "On your knees, man, forehead on the floor. When the queen turns away, rise quickly and leave the room."

Trembling, Daedalus lowered his tall self. What had gone wrong? The cold started on his forehead, but it seemed to travel through his whole body.

Later, safe in his own apartment, he thought he would explode in rage. He fought for control.

"What ails you, master?" asked Mena anxiously.

Daedalus raised his arm to strike her, then pulled back. He glared. "I've had my forehead on the floor in front of the queen, a slave's posture and a slave's gesture, Mena, though I would be ashamed to demand it even of a slave. I would not abase myself like that to save my life. I did it for my son." Mena's face grew pale. "It is your fault, woman. You failed to keep Icarus by your side."

"Perhaps I should come back another time," a woman's voice broke in hesitantly.

Daedalus swung to face the sound. Beside the open door stood the court lady in the blue gown, her flounces edged with silver. Daedalus raised his eyebrows.

"I'm sorry your audience ended badly," the woman's quiet voice continued, "and it's not my place to interfere if you are determined to beat your servant. All the same, the queen was bound to see your son one day, and the sight of him was sure to make her fly into a passion. Today or another day, what matter?"

Mena's hand went to her mouth. "It was my fault," she said wretchedly. "I fell asleep with the child, and he woke up and wandered off. But I do not know why it mattered so much. Can it be they don't like children here?" She gazed at the strange woman in mute appeal.

Daedalus was still crimson with anger. Absently, he picked up a slab of clay and began pounding it on a board. Both women watched, but did not speak. Gradually, Daedalus's face returned to its normal colour. His movements became less furious. He put down his clay and covered it with a wet cloth, then turned to face the visitor.

"Who are you?" he asked. "I abased myself in front of the queen like a slave because you said so, and now I wonder why."

"I'm Hebe," answered the woman.

"Cupbearer to the gods?" asked Daedalus ironically.

"No," Hebe smiled. "That's the other Hebe." The little joke had never really amused her, but she was glad of it now. The black-haired stranger towered above her, but he seemed no longer menacing. "The queen honoured me with her invitation to be present this morning," Hebe continued. "She knew it would mean a great deal to me. I'm an artisan in a small way myself." She bowed.

"Are you, indeed." Daedalus washed his grubby hands, all the while sneaking little glances at his visitor. Her eyes were ringed with soft blue, the same colour as her gown. She looked down, and Daedalus saw that her eyelids were painted silver. "What do you want with me?"

"To earn your trust," said Hebe simply, "and to learn from you, if you will permit me." Her voice was calm. "I know the customs and the people. I can help you. I want to be your new assistant."

"Really?" Daedalus nodded his head in the Greek gesture for "no."

"Give me a chance," said Hebe eagerly. "Here, these are mine. Look at them." She held out four seal rings.

Daedalus took them casually, then walked over to the window and bent over them. "You did this carving?" he asked. It was obvious he did not believe her.

"Certainly." Hebe flushed. "Why do you doubt it?"

"A woman! Who taught you?"

"My mother, who else? My father also. My family

38

have been carvers and workers in wood and metal for generations. Jewellers, sculptors, potters, sometimes a needlewoman or a weaver. My mother was a great artist, and artists are honoured at this court. Why are you surprised? Are there no women in Athens who do this work?"

"Needlecrafts or weaving, yes. Those are women's work. The others, no."

Hebe snorted. "And people call Athens a civilized land!"

Daedalus shrugged. His eyes fell again to the rings he held. The work was exquisite, each tiny piece meticulously incised. "You have a gift for it," he admitted.

"Let me help you, then," Hebe begged him. "Let me learn from you." Her smile was brilliant.

"Why on earth should you want to do that?"

"I'm a skilled worker in gold and silver," replied Hebe earnestly, "and my frescoes have been praised. But I long to make new things, Master Daedalus. I want to be an inventor, like you."

"Inventing is not something that can be learned. Either your mind works that way or it does not. I've been making things, as you put it, since I was a child. It did not matter if they were new or not, I had no way of knowing. They were new to me."

"How can I explain to a stranger?" Hebe was quivering with intensity. "I made things too, when I was a child, but always under my mother's eye, always as she instructed me, nothing different. This is an ancient culture, here at Knossos. We do the old things very well, and still in every generation we strive to do them better. Nobody even thinks about doing new things. Let me work with you. Maybe my mind will work the way you say and maybe it won't. Either way, we both gain. I will find what I need to know about myself, and you will have my good help."

"It's kind of you," Daedalus spoke formally, "but I don't want an assistant." After Talos, he would never want another assistant.

"You may not want an assistant," Hebe urged, "but you need someone here to keep you out of trouble."

"Trouble," echoed Daedalus. "Tell me, Hebe, what went wrong with my introduction to the king and queen?"

Hebe came forward and stood close to Daedalus. He stepped back involuntarily, then bent to catch her low tones. "Haven't you heard about the royal monster?" she asked.

"No." His voice was as quiet as hers.

"The queen's child. I've heard him called the Minotaur, the bull of Minos. It's a joke, a cruel one. He's a child who should not have lived, but he did live. There's been precious little happiness in the royal apartments since he was born."

"What's wrong with the child?"

"Club foot, no neck at all, horns on his forehead. A monster with a bull's head!" Hebe rolled her eyes.

"You have seen all this?"

"Of course not. Nobody I know has seen him since the day he was born. Stories go round, and they grow in the telling. Maybe they're all lies. Something is badly wrong with him, though. The king used to love the queen very much, and she used to love him, too. You could tell, from the way they looked at each other, or from their voices when they talked. They had a little daughter, nothing the matter with her. Then the monster. As the story goes, the queen showed a perfect child to the king, pretending this was the child she had borne. She tricked her husband into accepting the monster."

Daedalus nodded. "Sometimes a mother will do that. It's a dreadful thing for a royal family. How could such a creature rule the kingdom?"

"This one could not. He has never learned to talk, as far as I know. His sister is Ariadne the Most Holy. A child still, but she serves the Goddess. We had queens in Crete long before we ever had a king. I believe Ariadne will rule here after her father dies."

Daedalus nodded. We Athenians would never tolerate a female ruler, he thought. "How did the king find out the truth?" he asked.

"I was present." Hebe shivered. Daedalus raised his eyebrows. "It was at the festival of Poseidon," Hebe continued. Her eyes were bleak. "The king himself had sacrificed a magnificent black bull. He always sacrificed the very best animal in the whole of Crete. They say he cheated Poseidon once, and the monster was the god's punishment. If that is true, no punishment could be more cruel.

"Right after the sacrifice, King Minos sent for his baby son. He was still holding the great axe in his bloody hand. The priests raised aloft the great silver basins, filled with blood. What did the king intend to do? Did he think to dedicate the child to the god? What a mockery that would have been!

"The queen's carved throne had been set on a platform at a little distance from the altar, and I don't think she realized what was happening. The child was brought. I was seated with my mother among the artisans. Have you seen the place?"

"Not as yet."

"Tiers of stone seats look down on the altar below. I could not see the queen's expression, but I saw the king very well. He put aside the child's clothes. His face turned black. Whatever the king saw, he must have known at once that this was no normal child. The queen's slaves were executed on the spot. The queen rushed down like an avenging fury and snatched up the child, but she did not try to save them. I'm sure she saw it would be useless.

"The king wanted to expose the child, even though he had accepted it. He sent two priests to the cave of Dicte, where Sky-father Zeus was born, asking what he must do. Both men dreamed that Minotaur would be remembered after his father had been long forgotten. They warned the king not to endanger the child's life, but the queen has never seemed to believe her son is safe. It all happened years ago, but it's still a festering sore between the king and the queen." Hebe stopped. She glanced at Mena, who had moved to a corner of the room before taking up her distaff. Now she was spinning busily. However sharp her ears, Hebe was sure she could not overhear their words. She gazed up at Daedalus. "I am being very frank with you," she said slowly.

"You are indeed," Daedalus agreed. "I have been wondering why."

"I want to be your assistant," said Hebe, "and that will not happen if things go badly for you."

"I hate intrigue," Daedalus burst out.

"So do I," agreed Hebe, "but I think you will not survive here unless you know these things. I hope you will do more than survive." She reached out to touch his arm, but changed her mind and drew back awkwardly. "You may be able to help all of us," she said slowly. "When I watched you this morning, I saw the possibility. You distracted us. The king and queen laughed. Everybody was happy. I think we had all forgotten it was possible."

"Until my son arrived."

"How old is he?"

"Icarus? Halfway past his third birthday."

"The monster child is a few years older. Icarus is a beautiful boy. I am afraid the queen must envy you. She is a proud woman. She will be very angry if she finds herself envying you, a common citizen."

"A citizen of Athens," Daedalus replied sharply.

"You are not in Athens now," said Hebe. "You saw the queen's face – and the king's." Hebe shook her head.

"This is frightening," said Daedalus. "It's sad as well. Does the Minotaur live here at the palace? Who looks after him?"

"I do not know." Hebe shrugged helplessly. "The queen's private apartments were rebuilt after his birth. I'm told three or four rooms were furnished as a nursery. It's a big palace." She paused. "The king wants one thing, the queen another. Both of them may ask for your help."

Daedalus swallowed. "I must think about all of this," he told her. "Thank you for the information, Hebe."

He studied her face intently. If everything she had said was true, his life and his dear son's life might depend on her help. She met his gaze with clear grey eyes. She would not turn out to be an inventor, of course: she was a woman, whatever her skills. He would let her discover that truth for herself. He beckoned to Mena.

"If you are willing," he told Hebe, "you may come tomorrow to help Mena unpack our things."

Hebe shrugged. "I want to learn from you," she said, "but I'll do whatever is needed. I'll help Mena, gladly." She smiled at Mena. Her footsteps brushed the tiled floor, and Daedalus turned as the door swung shut behind her.

"That was wise." Mena tugged at a heavy bundle, struggling to untie its leather thongs. "I was afraid you were going to send her away. Here in the palace, many fine artists live and work, men and women both. They are honoured, and the work they do is valued. Stephanos and I have talked to people while you have been entertaining the court. Hebe is well thought of here."

CHAPTER THREE

A LABYRINTH
FOR A MONSTER

The king sent for Daedalus the very next day. This time the audience was private. Escorted by a youthful guard who carried a gilded javelin, Daedalus walked through an antechamber into the throne room itself. He glanced around him nervously. The room was low, not large, and dimly lit. A single throne, carved in gypsum inlaid with lapis and silver, was set on a raised platform. On the wall behind, a pair of painted griffins crouched. They were facing each other, as if either to attack or to protect the king, Daedalus was not sure which. The griffins thrust up their eagle beaks almost to the top of the throne. The tails of their lion bodies seemed to twitch. The king sat between the two beasts, his head again crowned with a cascade of white plumes.

"I'm pleased to have you here at last," the king began. "You know your work is admired in Crete, and has been for a long

time. This is my first opportunity to talk to you in private." He paused, staring down at Daedalus. Daedalus had been as tall as his father before he was ten years old. It was very odd, having to look up to meet anyone's eyes. "Are you a sensible man, as well as a clever one?" the king asked at last. "Are you a man to be trusted with a delicate job?"

Daedalus could smell danger. He was thankful for Hebe's frankness – if indeed Hebe had told the truth. His neck and back ached with tension. "I use the common sense the gods have given me, Majesty," he replied at last.

The king studied the black-haired stranger. He stared into the inventor's brilliant blue eyes. Could this man be trusted? How far? The king could not tell. However, no one else at Knossos was capable of carrying out the task he had in mind. He stared at Daedalus, but his mind was elsewhere, seeing again the monstrous creature his wife had borne. He blinked and focused on the man in front of him.

"Zeus has surely sent you to me," Minos said. "The Sky Father knows my need." He paused again. It was not easy to describe his need. "You must build a place of corridors and tunnels," said the king, "a maze where food and water may be supplied, but where no one can go in or out, except by my command. It must be so big, and so full of corridors, that no one wandering there can find a way out again. There must be one entrance, no more, and I must have the only means of opening and closing it. Most important, no one but you can know the complete plan of the place." His eyes were fierce.

"May I ask a question?" asked Daedalus cautiously at last. Minos frowned, but gestured him to speak. "Where is this structure to be located?"

"Here in the palace, of course," said the king, "or beside it, underneath it, as you recommend."

"It will be very large."

"Make it as large as the palace, if you wish."

"I have not seen the whole of the palace yet, Majesty, but I am told it is the largest building in the world. How many helpers will I have to build

your maze?"

"As many as you ask for, slaves and free men both. When the work is done, however, I must be assured of their silence."

Daedalus shivered. He stared at the king, fierce as a living eagle between the two painted eagle heads. A little muscle twitched beside Minos's eye. "I must see the palace first," said Daedalus at last, "and study it. Water must be supplied, you tell me, and food. I will make a design."

"That design must be carried in your head," said the king. "Don't draw any lines on wax or clay. Can you do this?"

Daedalus smiled. Probably no one else in the world could build such a plan in his head and keep it there, but it was exactly how Daedalus liked to work. Even for the most complicated project, he did not need to draw lines and record measurements.

"I can do this," he replied. As he spoke, he recognized a difficulty. "I can carry a great design in my head," he explained, "but I cannot depend on others to do the same with even a small part of it. If I cannot give anybody a plan, I will have to supervise everything in person. The work will go slowly." I'll have little time for my own work and less for my son, Daedalus thought. Icarus may be a man before this project is completed.

The king frowned. At last he shrugged. "The bull from the sea will arrange matters as he wishes. I am in his hands."

The bull from the sea? That would be Poseidon the Earth-shaker. What did the king mean? Minos tapped twice with his staff on the floor beside his carved chair. It looked as if the audience was over.

Suddenly there was a commotion. Queen Passifay strode into the room, her great skirts swinging. She stepped up to the platform and stood, erect and proud, beside the king. "You have moved quickly, husband," she said. "Once you would have spoken to me first." The king inclined his head gravely. "Tell me, Daedalus," the queen continued, "has my husband commissioned you to build a jail?"

"Your Majesty?" Daedalus chose not to understand her.

"A jail, a prison, a cage for a helpless child."

"He is not a helpless child," said the king. "You tell me his father is a bull. You tell me so, my queen, and I believe you. His looks are strange enough for me to be sure that no man was his sire, certainly not me."

His voice was quiet. His calmness seemed to rouse the queen to greater fury. She sucked air in, and exhaled angrily. Her hands closed convulsively and opened again. Daedalus saw red marks where her nails had cut the skin.

"You mock me, husband," she said bitterly.

"I?" he replied, without looking at her. "Not at all. It has happened before, and in my own family, as you know full well. Europa was loved by a bull – Zeus in the form of a bull – and he brought her to this very island of Crete to bear her children. She was the mother and he the divine father of my great ancestor, the first King Minos. Why should your son not be the child of a god?" He turned and stared at her.

"Wait here, both of you," commanded the queen. Her heavy skirts whispered down the steps behind her.

Daedalus looked anxiously around him. Despite Hebe's warning, he had not been ready for this! Should he have stayed in Athens after all? The king sat as if carved from ivory, almost as white as his chair.

They heard the sound first, a moaning cry. It went on and on. Did the creature never pause for a breath? At last there was a gasp, then the moaning again. Daedalus had never heard such a mournful noise. It rasped on every nerve. The queen marched to the base of the platform.

"Come down, husband," she commanded. "You are my husband, and this is my child. Come down and look at him." Minos got up. Slowly, cautiously, he descended. The queen turned to Daedalus. "You come and look at him too," she ordered. "The builder must know who will dwell in the building. This is my only son. He is called Minotaur. His fame is destined to outlive mine and my husband's too."

The king's lip curled scornfully, but he did not speak.

A woman carried the child. By her dress, she was a servant, but she carried the slight body as if she cared. Another servant bore a chair, and the woman, at a gesture from the queen, sat the child in it, supporting his oversized head against her belly. The boy's body was contorted, and Daedalus read intense pain in his mud-brown eyes. The women tried to pull the ungainly limbs into a normal sitting position, but the twig-like arms and legs immediately twitched into strange angles, and the enormous head went sideways, as if pulled down by the muscles of the scrawny neck. A thin hand scrabbled at the arm of the chair. The moaning never stopped. The speakers added volume to their voices.

"I see your son," said the king evenly. "He is little changed from a year ago, or was it two years? A bull's son should have been stronger."

Wishing the room was better lighted, Daedalus studied the boy. He seemed to have all the usual human parts, though not the usual control of them. The head was horridly misshapen as well as oversized. One eye was higher and bigger than the other. The mouth curved up on one side, but sank on the other. How unlike his own sturdy Icarus!

"Minotaur," said Daedalus. His voice was unexpectedly harsh, and he tried again, more gently, "Minotaur." The head barely moved, but the mismatched eyes met Daedalus's own, focused long enough for Daedalus to be certain that the boy had responded, then skittered away. A great wave of sadness washed over him. "I could build a cart," said Daedalus quietly. "Something with cushions and a headrest. It would be easier to move him. It might be that he could learn to move himself."

"Build it," said the queen.

"Build the labyrinth," said the king.

Daedalus bowed and turned away. He could already feel the tunnels begin to twist and turn.

ରେରେରେରେ

Daedalus spent two weeks exploring the palace. "Me too," Icarus begged, but Daedalus would not risk the queen's anger.

"Stay with Mena," he told the boy. "For your life, don't let him out," he commanded her.

The basic plan of the palace was straightforward enough. It was dominated by a great central courtyard, rectangular in shape, with the longer axis running north and south. Windows and balconies overlooked the courtyard, and columned stairways led down to it. Outside the west wall was an informal open court. Ritual and state apartments were in the west wing, while the private apartments of the king and queen were in the east, where an old mound had been excavated above a beautifully tended ravine.

Daedalus watched a partridge for an hour, enjoying the bird's strutting walk and its hurried, whirring flight, so different from the effortless soaring of a seagull or an eagle. Workshops of the potters, gem-cutters and other artisans faced the central court of the palace and were separated from the royal apartments by no more than a passageway. Hebe had not exaggerated when she said that artists were honoured here.

The scale of the structure was almost more than Daedalus could cope with. The palace covered nearly five acres. Much of it was three, four, or even five storeys high. Wings and storeys had been torn down or rebuilt with wild disregard for consistency, although the total effect was glorious.

Hundreds of people lived and worked in the sprawling structure. Daedalus interrupted administrators and judges, scribes and artisans, cooks and stonemasons. Where was the armour? Where were the swords and lances? Daedalus found forges and blacksmiths, but no one was making weapons of war. An ornamented labrys, the great double axe of Crete, was displayed in the queen's private apartments. Dozens of small golden labrys decorated walls in the passage leading to the great audience room, but these were ceremonial axes, not weapons. Everywhere, slaves carried one burden or another, bricks or building stones perhaps, for new walls were

always rising, and old ones were being rebuilt or torn down. When the noise level was more than he could stand, Daedalus plugged his ears with wax.

On the lowest level, where the mysteries of the goddess were celebrated, the rooms were dim and quiet, the passageways dark. Above them, room after room was brightly lit by windows which opened on to light wells; colonnaded verandahs looked out over gardens down to the ravine. The palace was already a maze of tunnels and passages.

"I don't know why the king wants me to build a labyrinth," Daedalus grumbled. "He's got two or three of them. All he needs to do is cordon one off." His grumbling was half-hearted, however; he was already possessed by the project. He set out every day at dawn, returning when the lamps were lit.

Daedalus did not repeat Talos's mistake. Every night he poured a libation to Hephaestus. More and more, he felt the power of the god working within him. The labyrinth he would build would be famous to the end of time.

After fourteen days, Daedalus faced the king again. Minos sat between the two griffins, his hands rigid on the carved arms of his chair. "You must begin work immediately," he commanded. "I have one hundred workmen and five skilled masons for you. Tell me when you want more. Remember, Daedalus, I count on you to keep the secrets of this building. Nobody will be allowed to leave the project. Except yourself, of course."

"Until the labyrinth is complete?" asked Daedalus unsteadily.

"Until the labyrinth is complete." The king's lips curved upward, slightly.

Daedalus had heard stories of royal tombs in Egypt where no worker left the tomb alive. He felt a surge of anger on behalf of his men, even though he had not met any of them yet. Why should free men be killed to keep this secret? Anger soon turned to fear. Surely Daedalus and his son would face the greatest danger. However, it would take years to build the labyrinth. Daedalus would have time to plan a survival strategy for himself and Icarus.

CHAPTER FOUR

FRIENDS

While Daedalus explored the palace during the day, in the evenings he began to make a cart. Hebe turned up regularly. She watched while Daedalus sawed wood and smoothed it for the platform, then she arrived with two well-turned axles and four exquisitely carved wheels.

"I'd have made them larger," said Daedalus.

"The cart should be low," Hebe argued. "The monster won't have so far to fall."

"He's not a monster," said Daedalus. "Not normal — he's got a huge head, and his face looks as if somebody put their hands on his ears and squeezed, not evenly. His mouth is twisted, and one eye is higher than the other."

Hebe shivered. "How can you say he's not a monster? May the goddess protect me!"

"He could not keep his eyes focused for long," said Daedalus evenly, "but I could read his feelings in them. His arms flailed about and he could not control them. He seemed to struggle and then to fall into a rage. Who knows why? If I had a body like his, I'd be in a rage as well. For the first few minutes, though, those eyes were watching everything, especially me. It's not something a man forgets. I'd like to see what that creature could do. He might give me ideas for my mechanical man." Daedalus had forgotten that the mechanical man had been Talos's project rather than his own.

Icarus refused to leave the cart alone. Daedalus added a handle, and Icarus kept Mena and Stephanos busy pulling him around their rooms. When they gave up, he knelt on the platform with one knee and used the other leg to push himself, or took the handle in his own small hands and pulled the cart around, banging into chairs, tables and walls.

"You'll have to build a cart for Icarus," Hebe laughed.

"Much too dangerous." Daedalus jumped to steady the shelf that held his precious models of birds and kites. With one foot, he shoved Icarus away. He built a headrest for the cart and lined the platform with a cushion.

"It's ready," he told the queen. "I'd like to see how it suits Minotaur. Can the child be brought to my rooms, or should I go to his?"

"Minotaur does not go out," said the queen. "I brought him to see you and the king. It was necessary at the time, but I was sorry afterwards. He moaned for weeks. Minotaur does not like strangers. He does not like change."

"The labyrinth will be a huge change," said Daedalus.

"Yes," the queen agreed, "but many years will go by before this change can take place. The child may die." She turned sharp eyes on Daedalus. "It will be well if the work goes slowly," she told him. Daedalus made no response.

Over the weeks, the queen changed her mind. Minotaur came to Daedalus's rooms once, and then again. Icarus was wildly excited. The cart careened into shelves and caromed off walls. Minotaur fell off three times in the first half hour, but he landed sprawling and did not seem to hurt himself on the marble floor.

The queen gave Daedalus an additional suite of rooms on the

other side of the corridor which led to her own apartment. A deep balcony overlooked the great central court. Daedalus leaned on the railing, breathing the heavy scent of jasmine, lemon and verbena. Below him, brilliant in the sunlight, fountains played amid the formal gardens and court ladies chatted, their tall headdresses oddly foreshortened by his point of view. The brick wall of the balcony had an open design, and Icarus happily began to push a sandal through the first hole he found.

Minotaur came to know this balcony very well. Eventually he visited these rooms almost every day. Poor Hebe! Daedalus was beginning to build the labyrinth, and was gone from early morning to late afternoon. Without anything being said, Hebe found herself in charge at home. "I came here to learn from a master," she told Mena, despairingly. "I'm not learning anything, I'm not even doing the work I used to do. I've trained for that work all my life, and I've worked beside my mother since childhood, but I'm afraid to pick up my carving tools. My fingers have lost their skill since I became nursemaid to a monster."

"You helped make his cart," said Mena. "What else might you create?"

Hebe turned away, but her eyes were thoughtful.

Daedalus came looking for Icarus not long afterwards and found the air full of music, sweet sounds followed by others so mournful and so beautiful that his eyes filled with tears. He stared in amazement at a section of wall lined with reeds and pipes of different sizes. Minotaur's head was supported by a sort of cradle fixed to his cart, so that his mouth was in easy reach of the pipes. He was pulling himself from one to another. It was obvious that he was creating the sounds.

"What is this?" Daedalus asked.

Hebe came forward, smiling. "That moaning made my skin crawl," she said. "I began to build a wind chime, something big and loud to mask what came out of Minotaur's throat, but I changed my mind. I wondered if Minotaur might be helped to make sounds that could give pleasure to other human beings. Once I got the idea, these pipes were not difficult to make."

"It's an invention," said Daedalus thoughtfully, remembering how certain he had been that no woman could be an inventor.

"It has already helped me to like Minotaur better," admitted Hebe. "My family has always served the queen. When fate called me, I had no choice but to help her son, but I used to wonder how Icarus could stand him."

Icarus adopted Minotaur joyfully, treating the slight, ungainly body as he might a pet hound, perhaps, or a doll. He hauled Minotaur on to the cart and raced up and down the long balcony. He arranged the thin limbs and balanced the ugly head against the headrest. He talked incessantly to the creature and patted it and stroked it, saying again and again, "Hush, baby, hush."

Hebe built other devices for Minotaur, improving them where she could. Weeks might go by without her seeing Daedalus, then he would appear suddenly, with a word or two of advice or praise. "Make the lever in bronze, not wood." "Those springs must be tied." "I can see that Minotaur's arms are getting stronger, thanks to your ropes and pulleys."

As time passed, Hebe noticed that Minotaur's eyes often followed Icarus and might remain focused for several minutes. Sometimes his limbs did not immediately contract when Hebe straightened them.

"I don't know what it means," she told Daedalus.

"Maybe nothing at all," said Daedalus, concealing a shiver of excitement. "Keep watching, Hebe. Try moving his arms and his legs as if he was using them. Flex his legs. See if his arms can hold a ball."

"Do you want to make Minotaur into a mechanical man?" Hebe teased him. "Is that why I must work with him?"

Daedalus shrugged. "Do it for curiosity, Hebe," he replied. "Invent other devices and see what you can learn. I'll help as much as I can."

Hebe worked on Minotaur's body for several hours each day. She rubbed his arms and legs. She flexed his limbs. She persuaded Mena to hold his skinny arms while she pulled his legs out straight. When Mena said, "He's much better, isn't he," she was absurdly proud.

"Working with human flesh is more difficult than working with silver or gold," Hebe told Mena. Sometimes she felt she was sculpting Minotaur.

This was not the life she had dreamed of, but Hebe found it deeply satisfying. It did not matter if she never made another thing for anyone but Minotaur. Nobody else could help the child as she could, and nobody else except Icarus truly cared for him. Minotaur stopped moaning all the time, even when he was not blowing into his musical pipes. Sometimes his eyes would light up. Occasionally he laughed, perhaps for no more reason than he had once moaned. Then Hebe's eyes would shine with joy, and she would thank the great goddess who had arranged her life and work so well.

As the months turned into years, Hebe almost forgot her dream of working with Daedalus to build a flying machine or a mechanical man. It would have been exciting to help Daedalus, but very difficult as well. He was so sure that no woman could be an inventor. He would not have listened to her; he would never have developed her ideas.

Now and again Minotaur's sister, Ariadne the Most Holy, came quietly and watched Hebe and her brother. She never said much. Her slight body was always stiff and formal. Occasionally, she smiled. The queen did not come, although Hebe fancied the royal shoulders were less tense. On feast days, or when Daedalus showed off a new toy, the king and queen laughed together.

∽∽∽∽

It seemed no time at all until Icarus was ten years old, then eleven. Minotaur had long since moved into the suite of rooms near Daedalus. The queen had put Hebe in charge of him and then had seemed to forget about him entirely. "She's just like she used to be before he was born. I can't figure it out," said Hebe. "I have learned to care about him, and she has forgotten him. Her own son!"

"It must be a relief to her, to know he is all right and she doesn't have to do anything," said Daedalus thoughtfully. "I don't think she cared deeply about him, except perhaps in the beginning, but she's a proud woman and a queen. She fought her husband for the boy's life. Now she does not want to fight. Things change. The king does not press me to finish the labyrinth these days. Sometimes I think the king and queen would be happy enough if it was never completed. I'm the one that wants to be done with it. It's an octopus, with tentacles on my entire life."

Icarus was sitting on the floor, listening. "Take me into the labyrinth, Father," he asked. "That's where my friend is going to live, isn't it. That's where you live now, it seems to me. I'm sure you sleep there more often than in your bed at home."

"Perhaps Icarus should be acquainted with the labyrinth," said Hebe thoughtfully. "The knowledge could be valuable."

"Don't be a fool," Daedalus growled. "The knowledge could be deadly."

"Not if the king never hears about it," Hebe ventured.

Daedalus glared at her. He worried for a month. Then his chief mason fell ill suddenly and died. What if Daedalus himself were to die? Might the king or (more likely) the queen shut Icarus into the labyrinth along with Minotaur? Daedalus had nightmares for a week. Then he taught Icarus a secret.

"In the darkness, no human being will be able to find a way from the centre of the maze through its tunnels and ladders back to the great entrance," he told the boy. "There is another way, however, dangerous but not impossible. A small underground stream carries fresh water to Minotaur's living quarters. It emerges as a tiny trickle far down the valley. A grown man could not escape that way, but a daring boy might do so, or a small woman."

"Could Minotaur escape that way?" asked Icarus.

"No," replied Daedalus hoarsely. "His arms are strong enough, but he cannot control them sufficiently."

"I would not escape without him," said Icarus flatly. "Could I get into the labyrinth by way of that stream? Will you not take me into the tunnels and let me see the place for myself?"

Daedalus shivered. He felt a sudden hatred for the work he was doing. "There is no entrance except by the main door," he said, "and I will never take you inside. This is for your safety, Icarus, and for mine as well."

That spring, fever swept through the great palace, felling more than half of its inhabitants. All work on the labyrinth stopped. Daedalus escaped the illness, but Icarus did not. Mena nursed him as she had nursed his mother, terrified that he too might die. Daedalus held his son's hot hands, jumped up and paced, then sat and held Icarus's hands again. "Go to your workroom, master," Mena finally told him, lying bravely. "Icarus is not dangerously ill, but you are disturbing him. I'll call you if there is any change."

On the long balcony, Minotaur pushed himself restlessly on the cart. His eyes rolled this way and that, more and more frantic as the lonely days went on. Once again, he moaned continuously. Minotaur was older now, and his moans took on a deeper tone, as of a young bull in pain. When Hebe pushed him over to his pipes, Minotaur beat at them frantically, until the whole apparatus came down with a crash. Hebe pushed the cart out of the way just in time. Minotaur gripped her hands and pulled her down toward him. The movements of his arms and legs were not well controlled, but over the years Minotaur had become strong, and he pulled her face close to his. He moaned on a rising, questioning note.

"Icarus is ill," Hebe told him. "Sick. That's why he does not come. Please be quiet, Minotaur," she implored. "Let me massage your legs." She reached for her bottle of oil. Minotaur flailed, and the bottle went over with a crash, the oil spreading darkly on the marble floor. The cart went dashing away, propelled by Minotaur's strong arms, and smashed against the wall. Minotaur pounded the wall with his hands until they bled.

Hebe sent for Daedalus, who sent for the queen. "You've helped Minotaur so much," he said. "It's time for the queen to see her son."

Minotaur seized his mother's hands in a flurry of wild excitement, pulling her down like Hebe. Daedalus soothed, and Minotaur gradually released his grip. "Amazing," said the queen. "I never believed the prophecy that Minotaur would be famous in years to come. I thought he would not live long, and would not develop strength. Now one can almost imagine he speaks." She drew Daedalus aside. "I must have a way to see my son," she said. "I did not expect Minotaur would actually live in the labyrinth you are building. Now I see that I was wrong, he will not die young after all."

For years, the queen had put Minotaur out of her mind. Now, old feelings of responsibility and distaste sat heavily on her shoulders. It would be better if the king never knew what she was planning, but she would do what she wanted and face him out if she had to. Her chin came up. "Make me a private way into the maze," she commanded. "You will be well rewarded."

Daedalus stared down at her. Once, he had thought she might ask, and had found a way to connect a narrow staircase, hidden in her walls, to one of the old passages, but he had long since concluded she would do nothing to interfere with the king's plan. Besides, he had told Icarus there was no entrance, except by the great door. He did not want to have lied to his son, even after the fact. "Pardon, Majesty," he began slowly.

The queen stiffened. "This is my will," she said. Her eyes glittered. The silence hung between them like an axe.

Daedalus hunkered down beside Minotaur. He looked up at the queen. "I will obey," he told her.

Minotaur's moans did not sound like speech to Hebe, but she understood the boy's problem. "He misses Icarus," she explained. What would become of Minotaur if Icarus died? Hebe worried about Icarus, but she worried far more about the child she had once called a monster.

The queen sent for her own doctor, who bled Icarus.

"The doctor in Athens bled my wife," said Daedalus, almost frantic with worry. "Perhaps she would be alive today if he had not."

"The fever will break tonight," said the doctor. "Trust me, I know my business."

Whether the bleeding helped or hindered, he was right. Daedalus and Mena sat up with Icarus, taking turns to bathe the fevered body. They spoke very little, being almost numb with exhaustion. Toward morning, Icarus sat up suddenly. His eyes opened and focused. His voice was weak, but the hectic colour had faded from his cheeks.

"Mena," he whispered, then his eyes moved and he saw Daedalus. "Father," he added, with a little tender half-smile, almost unbearably precious to the man who watched, "thank you for flying with me." He closed his eyes sleepily.

Daedalus caught his child to his breast. "He's talking, Mena, thanks to the gods. Surely the child will live." Tears dripped down Mena's cheeks. "What did he say, Mena? What was that, Icarus?"

"Flying with me." Icarus opened sleepy eyes. He smiled, and closed them again.

"Icarus, dear son," said Daedalus gently, "we have never flown together. I have never flown. Mena, is the child raving?"

"No," said Mena sharply. "Dreaming, most likely. I pray it is a true dream, sent by the gods. Let the boy sleep, Master. You'll see, he will soon be well." Mena pulled the sweat-dank linens off the narrow bed and made it again with clean, dry sheets. What with relief about the boy and excitement about the words his son had spoken, Daedalus found himself in a state of acutely heightened sensitivity, almost more than he could bear. In his mind, he and Icarus stood at the top of a high cliff. Great wings were fastened to both of their arms, but it was nighttime and the wings were dark. Daedalus could not see how they were made and how attached.

Icarus slept, waking from time to time to drink warm broth, throughout the day and all the following night. He woke up hungry. Mena nodded in her chair beside his bed. Daedalus snored lightly in the next room. In gratitude, he had made a libation of precious wine for Apollo, god of healing, before he finally lay down to sleep.

"Make an offering to the goddess as well," Hebe had advised. "She has great power here on Crete. Zeus also. Don't forget the Sky Father was born in the cave of Dicte, not far away." Daedalus had remembered Talos and poured a fourth measure of wine for Hephaestus. It is never wise to neglect the gods.

Icarus found an orange and staggered off to look for Minotaur. He still felt weak and dizzy. Hebe witnessed the reunion. So did Ariadne the Most Holy, who had come more often during Icarus's absence. Minotaur gave a scream of joy. The cart hissed over the marble floor, gathering speed. Icarus dropped his orange and threw himself against Minotaur, whose strong, ungainly arms wrapped around him and held him in an iron grip.

CHAPTER FIVE

DAEDALUS TRIES HIS WINGS

From the beginning, Daedalus saw to it that his labyrinth workers were well fed and reasonably well treated. "Go easy with the whip," he commanded.

The overseers were amazed. "It's the only way to get any work out of the lazy louts," one said.

"Try it my way," Daedalus suggested. "An extra portion of lentil stew for the man who does extra work! See if they don't do better. Keep the whip for the man who tries to stir up trouble, and then use it without pity." Another time he reminded the overseers, "Slaves are valuable. Take care of them, and they will last longer."

"Why bother?" asked one of the men. "Fresh slaves have more energy. The king can easily get more of them."

"Do it because I say so, if you can find no better reason," Daedalus commanded.

In spite of all his care, three-quarters of his workers developed fever. By the time

Icarus was fully recovered and Daedalus was ready to start work again, more than half the crew had died. Many survivors were too weak to hew stones or carry rubble. In great frustration, Daedalus went to see the king.

"The queen and her women have gone to make sacrifices to the goddess," said Minos. "These mysteries are not for men. However, I have made my own sacrifice to Apollo the healer." He paused, then continued carefully, "My far-off ancestor was that King Minos who was sent to the underworld to judge the dead. Perhaps he gave me my understanding of illnesses like this. A fever is like a fire. Give this one another month, and it will burn itself out. Then come to me for a fresh crew. For the present, don't try to do any more building. Now tell me, if there are no more fevers, when will the work be done?"

Daedalus hemmed and hawed, then admitted that the labyrinth should be completed before another year had passed. "I have not hurried you," said the king, "but I have not changed my mind."

For years, Daedalus had been starved for time to use as he pleased. Now he shut himself into his workroom from dawn to dusk, when Mena would batter at his door or Icarus would call, in a voice that sometimes cracked from a boy's treble into a dark baritone, that supper was waiting. "Put it by the door," Daedalus often said, and Mena might find it there, still untouched, when she went to bed. The vision of himself and Icarus with wings on the cliff top drove the inventor, though he was not at all sure that the two of them would ever fly.

Icarus was thrilled when his father came and ate with him. "How is your work going?" he would ask. "Have you made my wings yet?"

Daedalus would launch into technical details. His current problem might be the fabric ("Coarse cloth is too heavy. How can I make fine linen strong enough to carry my weight?") or the frame ("Birds' bones are hollow, that's why they're so light. I've tried to use hollow reeds. I should be able to design a rigid frame …") or the tail, or variations in the current of the winds. After ten minutes, or fifteen maybe, he would notice Icarus's eyes glazing and his head nodding forward.

"I want to help you," said Icarus in distress, "and I keep going to sleep."

"You can't help much," said Daedalus gloomily. "Talos always had good ideas, but you don't know a thing about it."

Icarus wanted to protest: You forget I'm not thirteen yet. Talos was older. Besides, you taught him. If I don't know anything, Father, it's because you have not taught me.

He said nothing. What was the use?

Soon after his thirteenth birthday, Daedalus invited Icarus to spend the day outside the palace. "Minotaur can do without you for a few hours," he said. "I need your help."

"Of course," said Icarus, with a huge, delighted grin. Daedalus put two long linen-wrapped bundles into his son's arms. "Our wings?" asked the boy.

"Maybe." Daedalus grinned as widely as his son.

For several hours, they walked side by side along a dusty, tree-lined track. Keeping up with his long-legged father, Icarus soon developed a stitch in his side. His muscles ached abominably, but he was determined not to slow down and not to complain, and the pain finally went away.

"How do our wings work?" he asked.

"Maybe they won't work, not yet. That's one reason I want you here, in case I crash. They're not wings, exactly, more like a giant kite, a man-kite. If I land safely, you can try for yourself."

Icarus was alarmed. "Shouldn't I go first? You can tell me what to do, and you can see exactly what happens. Isn't that a good idea?" If anybody is going to crash, he thought, it should be me. I don't matter.

"I'm heavier than you are," said Daedalus, "so I'll go first. If my man-kite carries me, yours should do as much for you. I want to feel the way wings and wind work together, sailing the air." He laughed, his face flushed with excitement.

"Great Hephaestus, help me to help my father," the boy muttered under his breath. "Let me learn from him."

The path began to rise, gently at first, then steeply upward through a rocky gorge. Icarus heard the surge and sniffed the kelp-salt smell before the rocks parted briefly to show a gleam of silver, far below.

"The sea!" he exclaimed. "Is that where you're going to fly? It's so far down." What if you hit a rock? his mind continued. What if your wings pull you under the water? He shuddered. He did not want to go first, after all. What if his father drowned?

"Stop worrying, I'm jumping the other way, not into the water, and it's not far." Daedalus was impatient. "Today is only the beginning."

Now there were few trees, but brilliant flowers everywhere – tiny purple irises, cyclamens, wild gladioli, anemones, and rock-roses the colour of whipped cream. Daisies, white, yellow and gold, nodded in a breeze that grew stronger as the walkers ascended. Suddenly they emerged on to the narrow plateau, looking down from the lip of a cliff to jagged black rocks rising sharp and dangerous out of the pounding sea below. On the landward side the cliff was smaller, perhaps four or five times the height of a man, no more. It felt high enough to Icarus, peering cautiously over the edge.

Daedalus unwrapped one of the bundles they had carried, revealing jointed rods and linen cloth as fine as gossamer. Icarus's fingers were all thumbs as he helped his father to lay out one huge piece of cloth and put one frame together. Daedalus gave him a black look once, but did not complain. By early afternoon, they had made a giant rectangular kite with a long tail and a harness in the middle.

"Will it keep you up?" Icarus stared at the flimsy thing. It did not look at all like wings.

"I believe it will." His father was calm. "Watch me very carefully. I'll jump off the cliff and lean forward, as if I were floating on the air. The wind will catch this great kite, you'll see. I can guide it by the way I move my head and tilt the weight of my body, and I'll glide down gently. When we fly from a height, it will be a long flight. Today it will be short." He lifted one side of the rectangle and wiggled it. "Tell me what happens to the tail. I'm ready, Icarus. Ask the Sky Father to support me."

He and Icarus manoeuvred the man-kite to the ravine side of the cliff top. Daedalus climbed on to a big rock. On the ground below, Icarus braced himself to hold the giant kite while his father tied harness straps around his legs and chest. The wind almost blew them off before Daedalus was ready.

"I can't hold it," shouted Icarus.

"Let go, then. Now," yelled Daedalus.

Icarus took his hands away and stepped back. In the same moment, Daedalus raised his arms and pushed off. At once the wind caught his kite-wings and tumbled him and them, so that he landed heavily in a tangle of linen. Icarus crawled forward and peered over the edge of the ravine. Below him, in the middle of a patch of yellow daisies, his father lay still.

CHAPTER SIX

DEAD MEN
TELL NO TALES

W hen Daedalus had begun to
excavate for the labyrinth,
he had found the remains of
an earlier palace, and anoth-
er, even more primitive, under that. Here
and there, an ancient passage had survived.
In the early stages of the work, his crews
had found two skeletons behind a fall of
rock. Daedalus had shored up and extend-
ed the old tunnels. He had built narrow
stairs here and ladders there, joining the
upper level to the lower one, making
everything part of his convoluted design.

Beyond the old palaces, his workers had
cut a web of tunnels into the solid rock.
Different crews worked on different parts
of the maze. Work sites were dimly lit by a
strange bluish glow, without any source
that the men could see. Daedalus had cre-
ated this illumination, and the men went in
terror of him because of it. "It's unnatural,"
they told each other. "The whole thing is
unnatural. Well, what can you expect? It's

being built for a monster that lives on human flesh."

In reality, Minotaur did not eat much meat at that time. His upper jaw projected over his lower so much that chewing anything tough was difficult, although he learned to grind meat between the great molars at the back of his mouth later, when he had no choice.

The workers did not know what Minotaur was really like. When one man told a nasty story, the next felt he had to make it more horrid, even if he scared himself as well as the others. However, the bluish light was real. The secret of it went to the grave with Daedalus. He never used that light elsewhere, and he never told another human being how to make it.

In spite of the fact that men of each crew were familiar with their section, no labourer ever found his own way out of the maze. His mates might hear the lost one's screams, near one minute and farther away the next. Each man worked as well as he could, rather than risk being dismissed before they were all led out together at the end of the day. In the end, the overseers had no need of whips.

As King Minos had predicted, the fever ran its course. When Daedalus returned to the tunnels after wrecking his man-kite, with his cracked and painful ribs tightly strapped, he began work on the central apartment where Minotaur would live. His heart ached as he thought of it. Now that he knew the boy, it seemed shameful that he should be doomed to live for ever without feeling the wind or smelling the flowers, never seeing sun or stars. What could be done?

In the centre of the labyrinth, twenty miners dug out a suite of rooms exactly like the apartment where Minotaur lived. As each room was completed, Daedalus painted bright frescoes on the walls, the same as on the walls above, except that the new colours were more brilliant. Duplicating the balcony was his greatest challenge, but eventually the men got the structure right and excavated a space beyond the wall.

Daedalus took fresh brushes and paints. He intended to create an illusion of sunshine and sky, with a few soft clouds, and of a garden, with fountains and benches where people sat and talked. At the end of each long day, he gazed intently at his work. Slowly, a copy of the palace courtyard took shape, but it had neither sound nor motion. The white-winged egret remained suspended in the air above the lemon tree. The slave never finished pouring wine for the high-born lady, whose jewelled hand never quite reached the golden cup.

At night, in his own workshop, Daedalus moved his new man-kites aside. Surely he could make something so that Minotaur's garden would not be eternally silent and still. He built a fountain, using the same ideas that had gone into the making of the toy with the birds and the snake, so many years before. The fountain was more difficult, since no human hand would pour water into the sphere and drain it out again, but in the end the inventor was pleased with his effort. When he set it in the labyrinth, however, the living fountain made a mockery of the painted scene that surrounded it.

How could he bring the whole scene to life? Daedalus started looking for all the bits and pieces of the mechanical man. "Where are the cogs and gears from your cradle?" he asked Icarus. "What have you done with the bronze body and the silver hands?" he demanded of Mena.

Icarus pulled out chests that had not been opened since they arrived in Crete. While his father painted in the labyrinth, the boy tore their home apart, searching. He found springs and cogs, gears and wheels, huge folded sheets of lead, small sheets of hammered copper, along with innumerable scraps of wood and metal, and some tools that he could not identify at all, although Mena recognized the first saw Talos had made and came very near bursting into tears when she picked it up. Icarus found the silver hands, but the rod from one of them was broken. He found the bronze body, but it had been battered out of shape. "The sailors likely dropped it on the trip from Athens," Mena told him.

"I'm afraid Father will be angry," said Icarus, gazing nervously at the shambles around him. He tried to sort out a few things and put away some others, wondering all the time how the contents of a box can swell so much when they are taken out.

"Zeus help me, and Hephaestus too," Daedalus swore when he saw the mess.

"I wanted to help you," muttered Icarus, with downcast eyes.

"That's just the help I needed!" snarled his father. His ribs still ached, and he was stiff from crouching all day on the floor, painting the scene in which the baby Hercules strangles a pair of pythons in his cradle.

"Tell me what I can do, Father," said Icarus, feeling numb.

"Nothing easier," Daedalus snapped. "Useless boy! Get out of here, and don't hurry back." He faced his son with eyes as cold as ice.

Icarus held back his tears until he was outside the door, but then they came, scalding his hot, unhappy face. Mena was snoring, but he did not really want to talk to her. Without thinking, he went to Minotaur, thankful for the little private way from one suite of rooms to the other, and curled himself against the awkward body. Minotaur was warm. His limbs, which jerked almost continuously during the day, were relaxed. One arm wandered across Icarus's shoulder, though he did not wake. Why haven't I ever done this before? thought Icarus, and closed his eyes …

Somebody was patting him and laughing. Icarus felt the warmth of the sun. He opened his eyes. Minotaur looked down at him. Icarus had never found the odd face repellent; it was Minotaur's face, just as Hebe's face was hers, but Minotaur had not ever looked down at him like this, so his face looked strange. Even more strange, Minotaur was laughing, chuckling. Icarus smiled back. Then he remembered, and groaned. Minotaur's face changed at once, reflecting terrible dismay.

"Oh, Minotaur," Icarus blurted, "I'm so unhappy, my father hates me." He stopped, horrified. In the beginning, Hebe had insisted that Minotaur did not understand anything, but Icarus knew better, even then. If he had not already known, one look at Minotaur's face would have been enough. Who had tasted – who had felt – more of a father's hatred than Minotaur? Icarus had already hurt his father; now he had badly hurt his friend. My father is right, I'm no use to anyone, he told himself. His despair welled up, ten times worse than before. With an incoherent cry that could as easily have come from Minotaur, Icarus jumped up and ran.

He did not stop until he was out of the palace altogether, walking along one of the streets of the city. It was a street of food shops, and the smells tantalized and beckoned, fresh honey cakes especially, his favourite. Three boys about his own age squatted in the street, rolling marbles against the front of a stall. Icarus eyed them cautiously, wishing he had been allowed out long ago. Maybe they could have been friends. One of the boys shouted suddenly, "What are you staring at, idiot?" Icarus flinched and ran.

Nobody wanted him, nobody could help him. He was "beyond human help." He'd heard that phrase a time or two, used perhaps of a man who had killed his wife, or a woman who had murdered her child. Soon, his feet slowed. Where could he go? Suddenly, he decided to look for a shrine sacred to his ancestor, Hephaestus. Surely the lame god would understand a supplicant who couldn't do anything right. On the other hand, maybe Hephaestus would be angry because Icarus had never thought of making a sacrifice before, and thought of it now only because he was in trouble.

In turmoil, the boy plodded on. The sun set and he stumbled before he realized that he was walking in the dark. He looked up, but could not see moon or stars to light him home. Mena would think he was with Minotaur again, and Hebe would be sure he was in his own bed. His father would not look and did not care, Icarus was sure of that. Shivering, he drew his light tunic around him and lay down by the side of the road. He pulled tall ferns around his body, but the wind chilled him nonetheless. He closed his eyes.

In his dream, Icarus held his hands to the heat of a divine fire. Hephaestus looked up from his forge. The god's face was alight with a terrible, cold beauty. It seemed to Icarus as cold as his father's face after Daedalus had dismissed him, and again he was numbed by despair.

"I never had a father," the lame god told the boy. "Why should I care about yours? Solve your own problems with him. I've no quarrel with Daedalus. It was Talos I destroyed, Talos who thought himself equal to the gods."

Icarus woke early, very cold and stiff. Had the god really killed Talos? In the chilly dawn light, the boy could see the palace clearly. He ran all the way. What else could he do? His father had gone by the time Icarus slipped back into their rooms. He was right, nobody had missed him. Who could he talk to about his dream? Mena? Hebe? His father? Icarus spent a wretched day.

Icarus's day was bad, but his father's was worse. "I had to tell the king that the labyrinth is finished," Daedalus told Icarus and Mena that evening. "I have not done everything I wanted to do, but the design has been complete for some time, and I cannot keep inventing work for one hundred men. King Minos went to the labyrinth with me as soon as I told him. 'Are all the workers inside?' he asked. 'And the overseers?' With his own hand, he locked the great doors. He has kept the key."

All thought of his own troubles was wiped from Icarus's mind. "What will happen to the men?" he asked. His skin prickled. "Have they got food and water?"

"Of course not," said Mena. "It's what you have feared for so long, Master, but I never quite believed it would happen."

"I did not believe it either, I find," said Daedalus wearily.

"They will die of hunger and thirst, Icarus. In a month or two, the king will open the doors again. Most of the bodies won't be far from the entrance. That's where the men have been working lately, carving symbols into the stones. They'll be trampling on each other to get at the doors by now. I'm sure some of them have been afraid of this, but they won't believe it. They'll pound until their hands are bloody, they'll bring their picks, the few picks that are left, but picks and knives will shatter against those doors." His voice lifted eerily, as if he were a poet singing a dirge.

Stephanos seldom came into their main rooms, but now he came, his face set and white. "The great doors of the labyrinth are closed, and a guard posted," he exclaimed. "Master, I thank Zeus and the goddess too that you are safe." Daedalus held out a trembling hand, and Stephanos ran forward to press it.

"They will not destroy me yet," said Daedalus. "Minotaur has not yet been shut into his living grave. I've done what I can for him, though. There's little enough time left for us. Mena, Icarus, make sure I'm not disturbed."

Feverishly, Daedalus worked to perfect his man-kites. He made bolsters roughly shaped like cocoons of himself and Icarus, and stuffed them with leather bags and rolled pieces of lead sheeting until they were the right size and weight. He had already experimented with diamond, oval and rectangle shapes for the glider-kites. He had tried long tails, short tails, and no tails at all. Now he had to make final decisions, with his own life and his son's life at stake. In the pre-dawn half-light, he flew his almost-final models with the dummy bodies strapped in place. Long afterwards, farmers and fishermen nearby would tell their grandchildren about monstrous creatures – griffins perhaps, or harpies – that had crashed into the sea.

CHAPTER SEVEN

A MAN
WITH THE HEAD
OF A BULL

A month to the day after the great doors had been closed, Stephanos came to the workroom. "The king opened the labyrinth today," he said. "My friend Thonis is one of the guards who pulled out the bodies. I helped to scrub him. What a stink! He'll have to burn the clothes he wore. So many men, all dead." He shivered.

Daedalus rubbed his aching eyes. Anger for the deaths began to burn in him. With a great effort, he forced himself to be calm. "I hope the king lights a good fire inside the entrance, to purify it. In a week or two, the worst of the smell will pass," he said. "I expect they'll send for me soon." He bent once more over a new harness, tying its wide woven bands to the latest man-kite frame.

The royal summons came ten days later. "You are to guide us to the centre of the labyrinth," ordered the queen. "I must see the place where Minotaur will live."

"And I must see the labyrinth," said the king. "We will dedicate it soon."

"Is it safe to go with them?" Icarus asked.

"No," replied Daedalus candidly. "Safe enough for the moment, though. The queen will protect me. I have information that she wants."

The king commanded his guards to wait outside the doors. Inside the tunnels, Daedalus stalked ahead of the king and queen. His white tunic glimmered with faint blue light, a beacon in the black darkness. Unnatural, thought the king. He was afraid of Daedalus, who could make light where no light should be. Fear was a new emotion for the powerful king, and it made him very angry with his guide. He seized the dagger at his belt, then remembered he was some distance into the maze and put it back again. This cuts at my power, he thought. I'll be sorry to lose him, but Daedalus must die.

Not all the corpses had lain by the main entrance. Sometimes the stink of rotting flesh assailed them, and all three walkers held their noses and swallowed down their vomit. Daedalus turned this way and that, passing dark openings on either side. The queen kept count for a while: three tunnels on the left, four on the right, turn right; two openings on the right, two on the left, turn left, down three steps and right again. Soon she lost count, and could not remember if the first turning was to left or right. Surely Daedalus himself would not be able to find the way out. Perhaps he intended all three of them to be trapped.

At last the light grew stronger, and they entered a passage whose walls were covered with bright, painted scenes. The king blinked as his eyes adjusted. He stared at the walls. "What have we here?" he asked. "Isn't this amazing! Daedalus, haven't I seen all of this somewhere else?"

The queen almost ran to the rooms ahead. "How is this possible!" she exclaimed. "Daedalus, you have worked a miracle here." She sat on Minotaur's narrow bed and held the soft coverlet against her cheek. For a moment, Daedalus thought she would weep.

The king pressed on past them to the balcony wall. "This is a wonder," he said, gazing down at the courtyard. Fountains played. The lady raised the golden wine cup to her lips and lowered it again. And again. And again. "Daedalus, the whole world would marvel to see what you have made here. It's a shame to waste all this on an idiot!"

The queen came to stand beside her husband. She hardly noticed his words. "Minotaur will be happy here," she said. "If he has Icarus with him, and Hebe to care for him, nothing will have changed."

Daedalus staggered. He leaned on the balcony wall with both hands. Icarus! Fool! cried his heart. Why didn't you see this danger? And Hebe too! He said nothing, but seethed helplessly all the way back to the entrance. Wild schemes dashed through his head and were abandoned: lead the king and queen into a blind alley and lose them? No. Try to bargain, as a condition for leading them the right way? No. Every notion led to a quick death for him and a slow one in the labyrinth for Icarus, and Hebe, and Minotaur. In sick despair, Daedalus accepted the royal compliments and watched the king lock the doors.

"The crescent moon is growing," said the queen. "In three weeks it will be full. We will hold our festival of dedication then. You Athenians do not worship the Earth Mother as we do, Daedalus, but you will be honoured among us on that day, Icarus too. Ariadne the Most Holy will not profane the mysteries of your people. We will celebrate your triumph when we dedicate my son to the service of the labyrinth."

To Daedalus's horror, the queen sent for Minotaur the next day, and for Icarus and Hebe as well. "Minotaur must live near the bull of his dedication for the next three weeks," her messenger explained. "Icarus must stay with him to keep him comfortable, and Hebe to care for him."

"I need Icarus to help me," said Daedalus, without thinking.

"Really?" asked the messenger politely. "When the queen has asked for him?"

Daedalus fetched the boy.

Minotaur, along with Icarus, Hebe and the bull, was very well guarded. "He's not used to open spaces," Hebe protested, but Minotaur did not go back to his rooms in the palace. Instead, a space in the arena was hung with walls of linen suspended from a wooden frame. Minotaur's small bed was moved inside.

Daedalus asked to see the queen.

"I had intended to send for you," she told him, dismissing her attendants with an imperious hand. "Show me my private way into the labyrinth."

Daedalus looked at her. Why should his feelings about Icarus matter to her? She had said many years ago that she would be grateful to him if he built the labyrinth slowly, and he had built it slowly. Perhaps she would remember her words.

"Help me, Majesty," he said hoarsely. "I have no other child but Icarus."

The queen listened. "You have served me well," she said at last. "Icarus must stay with Minotaur until the night of the dedication, but this I will grant you, your son shall not enter the labyrinth. Minotaur will be in his own place, and Hebe will be with him there. Icarus may remain with you. The entrance?"

"It winds down inside the wall of your own chamber," said Daedalus quietly. "You can come and go in secret, but only as long as no one enters your room after you have gone in, and finds the place empty. You will not use this entrance often?"

"Perhaps never." The queen stood up. "Show me now."

Daedalus followed her into the bright, spacious room. He hoped she would not ask how he had built this entrance. If she thought about it, she would know that he must have invaded her private space. This was the safest possible place for her secret entrance to the labyrinth, and Daedalus had done the work himself, but the queen might be angry nonetheless. Daedalus walked past her big low bed. On the frescoed wall in front of him, a stealthy cat stalked a large blue bird. The bird sat in the midst of slender, waving plants, totally unaware of its danger. Daedalus delighted in this scene; it had pleased him to make the bird's black eye control the secret entrance. He took a small wooden rod about the size of his finger, and pressed it against the eye. Inside the wall, a counterweight was released, and a huge block opened soundlessly.

"Take this ball of thread." Daedalus handed it to the queen. "It is thin, but very strong. Tie the end to this bracket. The stairs go down from here. Be careful not to trip! You must throw the ball ahead and follow it, then wind up the thread again when you return." He pushed gently, and the massive wall swung shut. "Will Icarus and I be permitted to leave the palace?" he asked nervously. It was as good as an announcement that he was planning to escape.

The queen raised her eyebrows. "My husband will not appreciate it if you do not return," she said. "He values your services. However, you have done what I wished. Take this ring." She handed him a copy of her own seal,

carved in amethyst. "It will be your safe conduct. Show it to the captain of the guard." Inwardly, she smiled. Daedalus and Icarus could leave the palace. It would not be difficult to bring them back again. She agreed with the king that they could not be allowed to escape.

I must be ready to leave the palace the night Minotaur enters the labyrinth, Daedalus decided. My man-kites must be completed and hidden beforehand. I must hire a small boat to wait near the base of the cliff and swimmers to cut us loose, pearl-divers perhaps, so that the wings which held us in the air do not drown us when we plunge into the sea. I'll warn Mena to watch her tongue and guard my door; the queen must not get a hint of what I'm doing. If the gods are kind, Icarus and I will glide safely down to the sea and meet the boat.

∽∽∽∽

Daedalus had taken little part in Crete's festivals since his arrival. Two or three times, he had watched the bull-leaping. Soon after he came to Crete, he had built a life-sized head of a bull, which automatically jerked from side to side as acrobats did headstands on the horns. Practice with it had saved many lives later when the same acrobats faced living animals.

At the festival of dedication, Daedalus sat on the stone seats of the amphitheatre. Where was Icarus? Would the queen keep her promise? Then he saw the boy coming toward him, pushed along by the biggest man of the royal guards.

"Here's your whelp, and I wish you joy of him," said the giant roughly. He gave Icarus a shove. Daedalus caught the boy as he tripped, and held him tight.

"Let me go, Father," said Icarus. "I must go to Minotaur. Father, I promised him." Daedalus felt his son's heart beating as the boy struggled.

"You can't go into the labyrinth," he protested.

"The priests knew I was going," said Icarus. "They blessed me."

"The queen will not permit it," said Daedalus heavily. "Sit down, the ceremony is starting." His grip tightened.

Icarus stopped struggling and sat. Somehow, his father had prevented him from going with Minotaur. But why? Daedalus had never come to the makeshift tent in the arena, and he had sent no message. Daedalus had been so focused on their escape that he hardly ate or slept, but Icarus knew nothing about that. The boy had got up every morning hoping for his father, and had gone to bed every evening in despair. He leaned against Daedalus, feeling his father's strong fingers bite into his flesh.

Below them the queen sat in royal splendour, alone. On a raised platform between horns of consecration stood Ariadne the Most Holy. The labrys, the great double axe of Crete, was supported on a stand in front of her. Golden snake bracelets twisted around her upper arms, quivering a little as her muscles tightened and relaxed.

There was a sudden noise like thunder, and a cloud of smoke. Everybody gasped. A slim figure in a golden loincloth stepped out of the smoke on to the platform beside Ariadne. He had a man's body, unmistakably, but he had the head of a bull! Daedalus shivered, holding his trembling son.

The bull head lifted. The bull voice roared, "Begin."

Through a narrow gate, the black bull was loosed into the arena. Daedalus looked at the bull, then at the bull-man, then again at the bull. The bull's hooves thudded on the packed dirt floor, sending tremors through the earth. Pairs of sure-footed acrobats took turns tossing each other toward the huge animal as he ran, seizing the long white horns as if they had been painted posts, vaulting on to or over the wide back, steadying each other when they jumped down. The crowd screamed at every graceful move. A team of women won the loudest cheers. Daedalus felt his head starting to pound.

Through the haze of headache, he stared at the bull-man. It's the king, I know it, Daedalus told himself. He recognized the slim figure. He recognized the loincloth. He was overcome with awe, all the same.

"Is that a god?" whispered Icarus.

"No," his father's light voice trembled in his ear. "It's the king. That head is made of leather, or of wood. He looks like a god, doesn't he." He felt Icarus nod.

In all his time in Crete, Daedalus had never seen the bull's head the king was wearing, nor had he heard of it. Had the king invented something new for today's consecration? What artisan had made that mask? More important, why had Daedalus not been consulted? Danger prickled his skin.

On the floor of the arena, the black bull's head went down at last, not in a charge, but in exhaustion. The acrobats stepped lightly toward him, and he did not move. They tied ropes around his neck and led him to the pillar of sacrifice, twice as tall as a man. The sacred laws of Knossos were carved into its granite sides, but they had long since vanished from sight under the dark blood of a hundred hundred victims. The women acrobats tied ropes to the bull's horns and held back its head. Ariadne the Most Holy raised the heavy axe and chanted its ritual, then handed it to the king, who swung it with great force against the animal's exposed throat. Two priestesses caught the steaming blood in golden basins and poured it down the pillar. The new blood ran bright red over the dark crust.

Priestesses brought the bull-child, Minotaur, pulling him on the cart that Daedalus and Hebe had made. Stooping, they anointed his forehead with blood. Minotaur sat straight, his outsized head supported by his strong back and arms. When the high bronze doors to the labyrinth opened, he propelled himself toward them. Hebe walked steadily behind the cart.

Icarus tried to get up. "No," said Daedalus roughly. "You stay here. I'm going." The tall man pushed through the royal attendants. His eyes met those of the gigantic guard and he ordered the man to keep Icarus in his seat.

"Make way for Daedalus," people shouted. Daedalus dropped to his knees in front of the masked figure. He was certain it was the king, but the figure had taken on height and splendour, and Daedalus trembled in spite of himself.

"Great One," he said humbly, "grant your servant permission to guide the bull-child and his servant to their home. Grant your servant permission to leave the labyrinth when the task has been accomplished."

Daedalus was no longer a proud Athenian. The king might shut him inside the labyrinth. The queen might have him killed if he tried to use her private way to escape. If he did not guide them, however, Minotaur and

Hebe would wander in the tunnels until they died. The blue light was already fading, except at the centre of the maze. Did the king intend them to die? Did the queen intend it?

"Your wish is granted." Inside the mask, the cold voice echoed. "Go, and come again."

Minotaur had reached the high bronze doors, and priests swung them wide. The cart rolled through, with Hebe following. Daedalus, on his long legs, was not far behind. The doors closed with a clang, and the day was gone. Daedalus took Hebe's arm. In the blue light, her clear grey eyes were serious, solemn even, but Daedalus could find no slightest hint of regret.

"Lead us, and hurry," she said. "The sooner you are out of this, the better."

"And you?" he asked.

"I did not choose this fate," she replied simply, "but I accept it. We are all in the hands of the gods. Minotaur needs me. In his way, he loves me, and I love him. Without me, I'm afraid he would really turn into a monster." She paused. "I have made so many things for him," she added. "I wish he could have his pipes."

Daedalus smiled. "That wish has been granted already," he said. "While you and Minotaur were being prepared for this ceremony, I moved everything. Some of it I had seen, of course, but much was new to me. You'll have to put the pipes back together – I had no time, Hebe, but all the parts are there." He shook his head ruefully. "You had so many clever ideas. That balance, with the plate attached, and the cup with a hole in the lid – have you made it possible for Minotaur to feed himself?"

"Certainly." Hebe looked up proudly.

"I might have paid more attention. You are a fine inventor, Hebe, and you did it with no help from me."

"I did it for love."

"Love? Ah – your love for Minotaur. Of course."

"Of course," agreed Hebe, with a mischievous twinkle in her eyes. The twinkle faded, and her grey eyes gazed steadily up at his blue ones. "You did help me, Daedalus, more than you knew."

"I hate this waste." The words exploded from Daedalus's mouth. He fought for control. "I have set up a workshop for you, Hebe. You can work if you want to. I have given you the best selection of tools and materials I could contrive."

"Daedalus, my life has not been wasted," said Hebe firmly. "Never think it! And with a workshop, and Minotaur, it won't be wasted here. Thank you, dear friend. Now quickly, lead the way."

The three of them moved along the passages almost as if they were going to a party. Daedalus and Hebe chatted brightly, although the pretence got harder as they continued. When they came to stairways, Hebe took Minotaur on her back. He was too heavy now for her to lift him in her arms. Daedalus carried the cart.

Soon, it seemed, they reached the centre of the maze. When they entered the painted corridor, the blue light grew stronger. The three were silent.

"Go back now," said Hebe. "You have used your greatest skill to make this life possible for Minotaur and for me. I know it. Now we must get on as best we can. Your duty is to yourself, and to your son." Her voice cracked, but she recovered. She seized his arms and turned him around, then gave him a little push. "Go now," she said.

Daedalus gritted his teeth and strode toward the doors, which eventually opened to the early evening light. In the arena, another team of bull-leapers had tied down another bull. The godlike masked bull-king stood as if he had not moved. The queen sat on her high seat as if carved from stone. Ancient gods, older than the far-off Olympians, surely ruled this place. Daedalus felt their power. Whatever their plan, he sensed that the building of the labyrinth and the dedication of Minotaur had been part of it.

The alien power lay heavy on him. Daedalus fought for breath, over-whelmed with sudden horror at Hebe and Minotaur's fate, and terrified for Icarus and for himself. As he watched, the high bronze doors of the labyrinth swung shut. The bull-man handed the gleaming key to Ariadne the Most Holy, who walked solemnly forward to work the lock. Daedalus breathed deep, convulsively. His head still throbbed.

The king's monstrous figure beckoned to him. "Today, we dedicate the labyrinth," the bull voice roared. "In the banquet tonight, we will honour the gods. Tomorrow is the women's rite. The day after, Daedalus, our feast will honour you."

Did Daedalus imagine mockery in the words?

CHAPTER EIGHT

FATHER AND SON

I've done all that was possible for Hebe and Minotaur." Daedalus looked firmly at his son. "Now we must save ourselves."

"If I go with you, Father," Icarus replied heavily, "I'll be deserting Minotaur." Minotaur loves me, he wanted to say. Minotaur loves me, and you do not.

Daedalus felt the words like a stone in his stomach. You are deserting Minotaur, he thought, and I am deserting Hebe. He swallowed hard. "Do you want to join Minotaur in the labyrinth?" he asked. "Is that your plan? You will never come out. I love you, Icarus." He forced the words out. "Do you want to abandon me?"

"Do you truly love me?" Icarus did not believe his father, but he longed to hear the precious words again.

Daedalus said them again. "I love you." He wrapped his arms around his son and held him tight.

The words vibrated through the boy's slight body. Icarus looked up at his father's face; the sapphire eyes were brilliant with tears. "I'll never forget," he said at last, "but my friend needs me, Father, and you do not."

"My only son? My only child? I do not need you?" Daedalus began. "How can you say that?"

He fell silent. In a dreadful way, Icarus was right. Daedalus knew, and Icarus knew, that visions of future inventions would always shape themselves in his busy mind. Whatever Daedalus might say, however much he might love Icarus, he would forget about the boy for days on end while the work possessed him. All the same, he could not bear to see the bright flame of his son's life dulled and quenched in the labyrinth.

"It's your duty to come with me," he said at last, reluctantly. "I'm your father, and I command you."

Icarus's face turned scarlet, as if he had been struck. "Father, that's unfair," he blurted. He caught his breath. "You kept me out of the labyrinth," he said angrily. "The queen changed her mind because of you, didn't she?"

He glared at his father. Daedalus did not deny it.

"Coward!" spat the furious youth. "Run away by yourself, Father, I'm not leaving." He stopped, shocked by his own words. He felt the blood draining from his face. Daedalus, staring at him, was also dead white. "Forgive me, Father," mumbled Icarus.

"Go then," said Daedalus, now icy calm. "Go into the labyrinth, the sooner the better. Tell the queen I release her from her promise. Ask her for the ball of thread to help you find your way. I wish you joy of your choice." He turned away. As for me, he told himself, I must learn to forget I ever had a son.

Icarus stumbled out of the room.

Daedalus almost fell on to a low couch. His arms and legs felt as heavy as stone. Was the boy right? Not right to say what he had said – no son should speak so to his father – but was the accusation well-founded?

Daedalus considered the matter, idly, as if it concerned somebody else. Was he wrong about his own danger?

No, not wrong, he concluded at last. He had seen his death in the king's eyes. Probably Icarus was not so much at risk. Daedalus had never taken him into the labyrinth. The king must surely believe the boy was ignorant of its design.

Take care what you wish, went the old saying, lest the gods grant your desire. Icarus would get his wish, to be shut up with Minotaur in the labyrinth. How many weeks would pass before he came to hate his friend?

Icarus was certain his world had ended. How could he have talked like that to his father? The labyrinth was no more than he deserved. Daedalus had said, "I love you," and in return his son had called him a coward. Icarus groaned. One minute he was convinced he must join Minotaur, the next minute he was equally certain that he must escape with his father and try to put things right. No, those words could never be unsaid.

Icarus slept fitfully, then paced about in turmoil. In the morning, he looked for Mena but could not find her. Perhaps even a servant like Mena had a place in the women's ritual.

Daedalus made a solemn libation to the gods, falling at last into a brief, exhausted sleep. No god sent him a dream. In the dawning, he carried the man-kites to the cliff and weighted them with flat stones. Icarus would never fly with him, but his father still tested every knot in his son's kite with trembling, hopeful hands. Perhaps Icarus had not meant what he said. People were always undependable.

How could he spirit the boy away? Now, when he most needed it, his agile mind failed to provide a single workable idea. He might make Icarus drunk. He could tie the boy and gag him and carry him, or get Stephanos to carry him. An unwilling or insensible Icarus could be brought to the top of the cliff. There all planning stopped. Icarus had to be alert and willing.

Even so, he might not survive the flight.

Icarus went to the big room in the slaves' quarters where Stephanos slept. It was a place to get away from his father. He could not risk seeing Daedalus after those terrible words. High, unshuttered windows on one wall gave a dim light, but Icarus had no idea which straw-filled mattress belonged to Stephanos. He had been there only once before.

At the far end of the room, two old men squatted over a game of bones. Icarus walked over. He waited politely, but they took no notice. He coughed. At last he spoke.

"Excuse me, please. Stephanos, Daedalus's man, where does he sleep?"

One of the players mumbled something and pointed a liver-spotted, bony, misshapen hand. Icarus swallowed his revulsion enough to thank the man and went where the fingers had pointed. He fell on to the prickly mattress, hoping he had the right one, and almost at once found himself sinking into sleep.

"Master Icarus, what are you doing here?"

Icarus blinked. Stephanos squatted by his side. He looks old too, thought Icarus gloomily. "I have to see the queen," he said. "I'm going to live with Minotaur."

"Your father's throwing his models on the floor and stamping on them," said Stephanos. "All the little birds we brought from Athens! Even the mechanical man! I said a word or two, and he turned on me. He's never beaten me before."

"It's my fault." Icarus began to cry.

Stephanos patted his shoulder helplessly. "Go to your father," he urged.

"I can't," the boy sobbed.

"If he does not leave the palace tonight," said Stephanos, "I doubt he'll ever leave it. The king has a nasty surprise for Daedalus, that's what I've heard."

"I called him a coward."

"You gave him a nasty surprise yourself, then. Now you're bent on staying. Your father has taken leave of his senses. I suppose he'll insist on staying too."

"He mustn't." Icarus sat up. "You have to make him leave the palace, Stephanos."

"I?" The old man laughed. "The day I make my master do anything, the sun will fall out of the sky!"

"You can do it," Icarus insisted. "Tell him I have gone into the labyrinth, you saw the queen unlock the doors, you saw me go inside."

"He may kill the man who brings that news."

Icarus beat his fists on the cold floor. "Tell him – tell him there is only one way he may come to save me, and Minotaur, and Hebe, and that is for him to escape now. The king will die one day, Stephanos, and the queen as well. If Daedalus is alive, he can return. If he dies, that's the end."

"The gods know the future, but we men do not." Stephanos sighed. "I'm not clever enough to make up that story, but perhaps the master won't

think of that. I will try," he said.

Icarus held out his arms. They held each other for a long minute. Then Stephanos got up and walked with dignity toward the door.

It was late afternoon before he returned. Icarus had no will to do anything. He had sat in a sort of daze for a while and then had fallen asleep again. Stephanos shook him roughly.

"Come with me," he said. "Your father left the palace an hour ago. Mena is back, you need to hear her news."

Icarus followed him, almost running, to their rooms. "What's happening?" he asked.

"Remember that nasty surprise?" said Stephanos grimly. "I had heard a rumour. Mena has found out all about it. The king and queen intend to take you and your father prisoner at the feast tomorrow. The guards have orders to put out your father's eyes and cut off one of your feet, and the queen's women have orders to tend you afterwards. When your wounds are healed, you will join Minotaur. Neither of you will ever get away."

Icarus looked wildly from him to Mena.

"Nothing is more certain," Mena darkly agreed. "Great people forget that servants have ears and tongues, or they think that any slave hearing such heavy news will keep quiet, out of fear."

"They'll cut off my foot!" Icarus looked down in horror. "That decides it," he said. "I must try to escape, Minotaur would want me to. Poor Minotaur – his parents are the monsters, not him. Do you think my father will help me?"

"He left this so that you could get out of the palace." Stephanos held out the queen's seal.

Icarus took it. He was crying again. "What will you do?" he asked, looking from Stephanos to Mena and back again.

"Don't worry," said Stephanos, "we'll be safe enough, nobody pays attention to slaves."

Tearfully, Mena held out her arms, and Icarus embraced her, then quickly pulled away.

"I'll never forget you," he said.

∽∾∽∾

The rising moon was less than half full, but the sky was clear. Daedalus trudged along. He had almost reached the cliff when his keen ears picked up the sound of running feet. He rolled into the shadows, eyes and ears straining, the smell of verbena and sage filling his nostrils.

"Who's that?" he muttered. "Can the guard be following me?" Then he saw Icarus. "Great gods of Olympus, I thank you," he breathed.

"Father!" Now that he had found Daedalus, Icarus hung back. In the moonlight, the man held out his arms, and the boy ran into them.

"Surely the gods have sent you," Daedalus said, marvelling. "Don't try to explain, dear son, you can do that later. Let me hold you. Oh, Icarus, I thought I would never hold you again."

Icarus felt his father's tears — or were they his own? He and Daedalus clung to each other.

Icarus found his voice at last. "Can you ever forget what I said, dear Father? Horrible words, I wanted to cut out my tongue."

"Be thankful you didn't," said Daedalus quickly. "I am." His arms closed tighter around his son, then dropped. "You are flying with me, aren't you?" he said. "You aren't going back again?"

"If you'll have me, Father." Icarus had never felt so much emotion in his father; it made him shy. "You were right about the danger," he said. "You were right, and I was wrong."

"Come then," said Daedalus tenderly.

In the silvery light, the little path beckoned toward the crag where he had left the two man-kites. They were roughly rectangular in shape, the biggest he had made, with the bottom edge swept back in the middle to a point. High winds always swirled around the cliff. What fate was waiting? He and his son were in the hands of the gods.

Daedalus put his hands on the boy's shoulders. "Listen, Icarus," he warned. "When we launch ourselves, don't let the winds carry you up into the sky. Gulls ride on currents of air to the heavens or to the earth, but we are not gulls. You must lean forward and float. Keep your head up at first, then bend forward a little. If you do exactly what I say, you will glide down to the sea. You are lighter than I am, it will be easier for you." If the gods are kind, if the winds don't catch us, he muttered under his breath, remembering with sick horror how Talos had been killed. "Don't get into a dive," he cautioned. "Don't roll over. Don't let yourself start to spin. Look for the boat, and glide in that direction."

"Head up, glide down, don't dive, don't roll, don't spin," repeated Icarus. "Look for the boat." How could he remember all of that, let alone do it? Head up, glide down ... he would do his best.

"Men have flown before," said Daedalus. "Perseus borrowed winged sandals from Hermes. Bellerophon rode a winged horse."

"Men have never made their own wings," said Icarus. "I'd rather have your man-kite than anything the gods could lend us."

"Careful what you say!" warned his father. "It's true, however, no god has offered us sandals or a horse. If we live, Icarus, we'll have done something no mortal has done before."

"Whether we live or die," said Icarus slowly, "surely we'll have done something no mortal has done before."

Daedalus's smile was luminous. He rested a hand lightly on his son's head.

"That's true, and we'll have done it together. We may be going to our death, my son. These wings may fail. But we will go down to Hades knowing what it is like to fly. Are you ready?"

"Yes," replied Icarus, with shining eyes. "Whatever happens, Father, I'm proud to wear your wings."

"I love you, my son," said Daedalus, his voice breaking.

He cleared his throat. To his left and in front of him the sky was brightening. He looked down at the waves that surged and crashed below. On his right, the sun's rim suddenly showed gold.

"Jump!" commanded Daedalus. "Now, together."

In a great leap, father and son launched themselves into the air.

EPILOGUE

The old stories say that Daedalus survived the flight and found refuge in Sicily. The Minotaur lived on in the centre of the labyrinth, becoming more and more monstrous as the years went by. His jaws became stronger. In the absence of other food, he lived on raw flesh and learned to like the flesh of human beings. Preserved by one Athenian, Daedalus, he was killed at last by another, Theseus, who used the queen's ball of thread to find his way out of the labyrinth again.

Icarus, alas, did not survive, or so the stories tell us. In those stories, Daedalus made wings of feathers, fastened with wax, for himself and his son. Icarus disobeyed his father's instructions. He flew too high, and the sun melted the wax.

Icarus could not really have died that way unless the gods had intervened, and the story gives no hint that they either helped or hindered. In scientific fact, for several miles above the earth the temperature falls about one degree Celsius for every 500 feet of altitude. If a human being could fly with wings made of wax and feathers, and Icarus had really flown higher than his father, he would have been colder, not hotter. The story of the sun melting the wax is clearly mythical, a warning to humans about the deadly danger of being too proud. The Greeks were fond of such warnings. Many old stories carry a version of this message. So the death of Icarus may be myth also. Perhaps the first teenager to soar into the air and ride the current of the winds did follow his father and land safely in the sea, to be picked up by the waiting boat.

AFTERWORD

Apollodorus is my main ancient source for the Daedalus story, and many events that form the base for my account were reported by him: Daedalus's murder of his nephew Talos, and his trial and condemnation in Athens; his flight to Crete, and his service there to King Minos and Queen Pasiphaë; the building of the labyrinth to house the Minotaur; and the construction of wings to escape from Crete.

I present a Minotaur very different from the classical monster with a human body and a bull's head, and my Icarus is his dear friend. My re-creation shows events and people from the old story in new guises, and puts flesh on old bones, though I like to believe myself true to the ancient tale.

∞∞∞∞

Classical scholars make the following distinction between myth and legend. A *myth* is a sacred narrative which explains things that a society cannot explain on the basis of natural law as they know it. A *legend* has some basis, however remote, in fact. In these terms, the tale of Daedalus and Icarus has elements of both myth and legend – the waxen wings and melting sun belonging to myth, and the airborne escape of a great inventor to legend.

Did any of this story really happen? Did any of these people really live?

Legend presupposes that some version of it did happen, though the details are lost. Daedalus did not sign his work. No doubt some owners in

ancient times were proud to ascribe a fresco or a sculpture – or a building – to his clever hands. His deeds and his fame were multiplied over time, and were enshrined by ancient authors in various tales about a genius inventor/creator/builder named Daedalus, or Daidalos, first maker of the axe, the wedge, the carpenter's level and sails for ships. His nephew (or cousin) Talos/Calos/Perdix invented the compass and the saw, and Daedalus was blamed for killing him out of jealousy.

Many kings of ancient Crete were named Minos. The great palace of Knossos was destroyed several times, partly or completely, by earthquakes. The vast ruins probably bewildered Greeks from the mainland, who did not build anything so big or complicated. Out of their awe and confusion grew the legend of the labyrinth, home of the *labrys*, the royal Minoan double-headed axe.

The bull was a Cretan cult animal. Magnificent frescoes survive that show acrobats vaulting over running bulls. Ariadne the Most Holy was worshipped as a human manifestation of the great goddess.

How do we know all this?

Two kinds of sources exist: literary and scientific. Of the Greek authors, Apollodorus is the best ancient source for the part of the Daedalus story that I have used, though I also consulted Pausanias and Ovid, the Roman poet who shaped the story as it is generally known.

All three authors told things differently, as, for example, in the "flight" of Daedalus and Icarus from Crete. Apollodorus gave bald details of their

escape by means of wings Daedalus had built. Daedalus warned his son not to fly high, lest the sun should melt the glue, nor too low, for fear of dampness from the sea, but Icarus failed to steer a middle course.

According to Pausanias, Daedalus built boats for the escape and devised sails, "an invention as yet unknown to the men of those times," so that he and Icarus could outstrip the oared ships of King Minos. There were no wings. Icarus, a clumsy helmsman, capsized his boat.

Ovid told a more elaborate version of the story. A modern reader might replicate the feathered wings Ovid describes, though if Daedalus had really made such wings, neither he nor Icarus could have flown with them. In Ovid's sentimental story, Daedalus found and grieved over the body of his disobedient son, although both Apollodorus and Pausanias say that Hercules found the body of Icarus and buried it.

Modern scientists and scholars make reconstructions based on evidence. Archaeologist Jacquetta Hawkes studied the ruins of Minoan Crete, among them Knossos, as a basis for describing Minoan culture. Like mythographer Joseph Campbell and paleontologist/archaeologist Charles Pellegrino, Hawkes makes a case for female power in ancient Crete – power that may or may not have been shared with men.

The Minoans were not warlike people. Cretan cities were not fortified; it seems they did not attack each other. No great armory was found in the ruins of Knossos. The Minoan rulers established a thriving and prosperous trade by sea, and they policed the sea routes to keep them safe from

pirates, but they did not use their sea power to conquer other lands. Minoan homes were full of light and open space. Minoan art featured women and men in various activities, neither subordinate to the other; it did not celebrate war or individual combat. Female figures of power – priestesses or queens – appear in frescoes and sculptures. Worship of the goddess continued in Crete and was eventually blended with worship of the male-dominant Olympian gods. Perhaps, in the same way, Cretan queens came to share their power with kings.

According to Charles Pellegrino, Minoan civilization ended abruptly in 1628 BC, when a volcanic eruption on the island of Thera dumped a layer of volcanic ash over much of Crete, smothering plants, animals and people, and sending forth tidal waves or *tsunamis* the height of skyscrapers, which moved debris from the ocean and left it sometimes two hundred feet or more above sea level.

Pellegrino describes teacup-shaped vessels engraved with bullfight scenes where the conquered bull has been snared in ropes. Similar scenes appear on the palace walls at Knossos. According to Plato, the captive bull was led to a pillar on which the laws of the land were inscribed, and its throat was cut so that the blood fell on the sacred inscription. Plato was writing about the mythical land of Atlantis, possibly Thera before its destruction. I have moved the pillar to Crete.

Pellegrino believes that Daedalus's wings must have been some form of hang-glider. Stories from India support this belief. They tell of ancient

Greek engineers who built gliders that flew well, although there is no evidence that these gliders ever transported human beings.

Peter James and Nick Thorpe are co-authors of *Ancient Inventions*, where the water-driven gadget featuring the snake and the birds is described and illustrated. It belongs to a later period than the one I describe, but similar toys may well have existed earlier. The palace at Knossos featured very sophisticated plumbing, including water pipes, sewers and flush toilets, as well as fountains. Daedalus, who is said to have installed the system, evidently knew a great deal about the uses of water power.

I have simplified spellings of some names for ease in reading. Daidalos and Ikaros are Hellenized spellings; Daedalus and Icarus are Anglicized versions. None of the stories gives a description of Daedalus. I have patterned my version of him physically, and to some extent emotionally, after Nikola Tesla (1856–1943), an extraordinary inventor and a pioneer in the field of high-tension electricity, who deserves to be better known.

BACKGROUND READING

Web sites for browsing:

Daedalus:
http://www.perseus.tufts.edu/cgi-bin/encyclopedia?entry=Daedalus
provides links to Daedalus references in Apollodorus, Herodotus and
Pausanias. Use the links to go to a module of text. (Some of the references
are more interesting than others. Try clicking on Apollod. vol. 2.121.)
Use the same URL, changing only the name at the end, to browse other
references, such as Icarus, Minos, Pasiphae (this spelling) or Minotaur; or
to find information about the life and works of Apollodorus and Pausanias.
These URLs lead the browser to Web sites of:

THE PERSEUS PROJECT, an Evolving Digital Library on Ancient Greece
(copyright). Home page: http://medusa.perseus.tufts.edu
This is an exciting cooperative project undertaken by classical scholars to
make specialized resources widely available for Web browsing or purchase
on CD-ROM.

CRANE, Gregory R., ed. The Perseus Project,
http://www.perseus.tufts.edu, March, 1997.

Books:

CAMPBELL, Joseph. *The Masks of God: Occidental Mythology.* Penguin, 1964. Volume 3 of Campbell's monumental work explores the worship of the goddess in ancient Crete and comments on the "particular accent on the role of the female" there, including details of the ritual killing of bulls.

CHENEY, Margaret. *Tesla: Man Out of Time.* Dorset Press, 1981. Biography of an eccentric, enigmatic modern genius.

HAMILTON, Edith. *Mythology.* Little, Brown, 1942. A readable and generally available account for non-specialist adults. Pages 192–4 give the Daedalus story as told by Apollodorus, whose version of it Hamilton prefers to that of Ovid.

HAWKES, Jacquetta. *Dawn of the Gods: Minoan and Mycenaean Origins of Greece.* Random House, 1968. Contrasts the more "feminine" Minoan with the male-dominant Mycenaean culture that succeeded it. Includes forty-five magnificent colour plates as well as many black-and-white photos.

JAMES, Peter, and Nick Thorpe. *Ancient Inventions.* Ballantine Books/Random House, 1994. Dispels the myth that all ancient societies were primitive ones.

OVID. *The Metamorphoses of Ovid.* Translated and introduced by Mary M. Innes. Penguin, 1955. Most accessible of the ancient literary sources. Ovid (43 BC–17 AD) wrote his version of the Greek and Roman transformation stories in Rome.

PELLEGRINO, Charles. *Unearthing Atlantis: an Archaeological Odyssey.* Vintage Books/Random House, 1993. A powerful exploration of the impact of volcanic eruptions, especially the one that destroyed the island of Kalliste (the "most beautiful"), leaving its remains to be called Thera ("fear").

ROSE, H.J. *A Handbook of Greek Mythology.* 6th ed., Penguin, 1991. An authoritative sourcebook for scholars.

DATE DUE

MAY - 4 2005	
MAY 1 0 2005	
JUN - 7 2005	
AUG 3 0 2005	
NOV 3 0 2005	
MAR 2 5 2006	
JUN 1 0 2006	
AUG 1 1 2006	
AUG 2 9 2006	

GAYLORD   PRINTED IN U.S.A.